Where did you come from,
Baby Dear? Out of the
everywhere, into the here.

—George MacDonald

MIRACLES &
MYSTERIES
of MERCY
HOSPITAL

Where Mercy Begins
Prescription for Mystery

MIRACLES & MYSTERIES
of MERCY HOSPITAL

Prescription
for MYSTERY

RUTH LOGAN HERNE

Guideposts

Prescription *for* MYSTERY

Shifting Winds Home for Erring Women

May 1890

I came here with the knowledge that anyone can make a mistake. As a woman, I understand this. As a midwife, I pledge to the Lord Almighty that I will do everything in my power to treat my patients, these young and not-so-young mothers, with love and respect.

Some fear the inevitable. A baby. A child. A new being.

Wait, that's wrong.

Most fear. They fear the unknown, the ostracization, the scorn, the indignity. Some were willing partners. Others were most unwilling, but the end result is an impending child in unconventional circumstances in an era of right is right and wrong is wrong.

Of course that's ridiculous, isn't it?

I—

A knock on the door interrupted Helen's journaling. She tucked the small bound book beneath her mattress, stood, and crossed the room. When she opened the door, nine-year-old Miriam faced her with a smile so sweet that Helen's heart ached with joy. "You've finished your lessons, precious?"

Miriam's eyes danced with happiness, a testament to her extroverted nature. "I have, and Miss Delancey offered me a caramel chew and it was most delicious. Possibly the most delicious thing I've ever had!"

"Thank you, Delancey." Helen smiled at the pregnant woman. "You are an absolute treasure."

Delancey set one hand atop her swollen middle. "Not many would make that correlation, Mrs. Davis."

Helen Davis, the name she used in her job here at Shifting Winds. It felt odd, hearing it, but it felt normal enough to inspire a natural response. "That would be their loss, Delancey. Was Miriam a proper student?" She shifted a brow in teasing question, because Miriam was always a proper student.

"She was and is, and Dr. Wellington's children learn as much from her as they do from me. She sets the bar high and is a fine example for those younger."

"Cora was a handful today," Miriam declared as she stepped into the room. "But little Jacob was good as gold. His papa calls him a gentle child, but he always says it with a look like this." Miriam drew her brows into a worried frown. "But why would being a gentle child be a bad thing?" she asked as she settled her books onto a small hearthside table. "He's little, but he pays attention, and that's a good thing, isn't it?"

"It is." If Jacob was the calm, Cora was the storm, and Helen found it funny that the roles were so antagonistic.

Their father was not amused by the differences, however, although Robert knew better than most that a gentle boy could become a wonderful father and leader, just as much as a robust counterpart. His own gentle nature drew people to him, and that made him an even better pastor.

"Jacob is a delight," said Delancey. "Cora is too, but she needs steering and there's nothing wrong with that. Both normal. But both quite themselves."

"They are that. Thank you, Delancey. And you're feeling fine?" Helen longed to say more, but she refocused the conversation. She was here as a midwife and housemother. To share too much opinion or confidence with the women and girls making Shifting Winds their temporary home set the wrong precedent. Long after they were gone, she'd be here, delivering babies and tending new mothers. She would be friendly and kind to the patients but not a friend, and that was a big difference.

"I feel huge, and I don't think that will be alleviated for some time yet," Delancey said softly. "And then I must think on what to do. How to take care of myself. And how to take care of my child."

"We pray." Helen put a gentle hand on Delancey's arm. "We take God's guidance in our hour of need, and we do the best we can because that's really all we can do. What the Lord puts on your heart will strengthen the soul."

Delancey bit her lip.

She'd told Helen her story when she sought shelter. Some sought quick confession as they came through the doors. Others waited a long while to speak, and some never spoke of their circumstances at all. If they ignored it, the problem would alleviate itself eventually.

"My soul magnifies the Lord," whispered Delancey, quoting the beautiful verse of Mary, the mother of God. "And I smell something slightly overdone in the kitchen, so I think I'll head down and see if Colleen needs help. I'm not on kitchen duty, but I'd prefer to keep busy. Good night, Miriam."

"I'll see you tomorrow!" Miriam sang the words brightly. When Delancey had disappeared down the long hall, Miriam went right back to her books. Her work.

She never asked about the home. Not yet, anyway. Did she wonder about all these pregnant women?

Clearly not.

For her, being surrounded by the fruits of a sensual society seemed normal. Helen wasn't sure if that was a smart idea or not. But it was their normal, and a beautiful mission. As long as she maintained it that way, Miriam would turn out fine. Just fine.

Chapter One

"YOU MANAGED TO DRAW THE short straw this morning, girlfriend." Shirley Bashore lifted her brows in sympathy when she spotted Anne Mabry in the far back corner of the archived records room on Tuesday morning, a spot she often referred to as the Vault.

Anne wasn't working in the normal records room. That would be bad enough on a sweltering muggy day like today. The mountainous files gulped the scant AC that permeated these back rooms, leaving hot, sticky remnants at human level.

Nope.

Today Anne was in the broad, windowless room that rational people avoided like the plague because it took hot and humid to new heights. "Aurora has a bee in her bonnet about an article in the *Charleston Buzz* that referenced deficient early medical care in our sweet city, and she wants me to find facts to refute it."

"Do we care?" asked Shirley. Her tone made it quite clear that she didn't.

"Not in the least," Anne admitted with a wry smile. "The point of the article was to champion the new Gaylord Cancer Center Infusion Wing opening next week, but you know how historians are," she went on. "Aurora doesn't just coordinate Mercy Hospital volunteer efforts, she oversees the volunteer fundraising drives for a multitude of events. And when it comes to history and our fair city"—she did a snappy imitation of a cheeky military salute, then sighed—"no one crosses Aurora Kingston. Which means that the new editor of the weekly best not get in the way, having been born and bred in New York City."

"So the editor's new in town? Like me?" asked Shirley. She'd recently returned home to Charleston from Atlanta to look after her mother. Regina Bashore had been a registered nurse at Mercy Hospital for decades before her retirement.

Anne went full-bore Southern, knowing the Charleston-born-and-raised nurse would understand her. "Why, shugah, she's only been here forty-three years. Her daddy came south when manufacturing took a downturn in the North. By our standards that makes her a newcomer. She could live to see ninety-plus years and she'd still be considered an import, Shirley. A Northerner. You know that," she said with a wink. "If she has grandchildren born here at some point, they might have a shot at being natives."

Shirley folded her arms across her chest and rolled her eyes. "Anne, I can't even imagine the day when the good Lord gives me time to fuss about such things. I'm on my way down the hall to get iced coffee, and I knew you were trapped. Can I get you a nice tall latte or sweet tea?"

That was the first thing Anne had learned about Shirley when she came on board in April. She went out of her way to be kind, and that endeared the African American woman to the rest of the crew working Mercy Hospital's main floor between the emergency room, the beautifully renovated main lobby, and the historic arm of Mercy Hospital known as the Angel Wing. When the historic hospital had suffered a devastating mid-nineteenth-century fire, the only wing that had survived was the one nearest the locally well-known angel statue. The wing had been modernized and refurbished, but the history and the statue remained intact. The summer had started on a rocky note with the statue's disappearance, but it was now back in its rightful place, and that was a good thing. Mercy Hospital hadn't felt right or whole without it.

"A latte, please," she told Shirley. "As big as they've got, short on ice, heavy on espresso. I've got to get this stuff found, and an ice-cold coffee would hit the spot. On the plus side, Addie is at camp until a week from Sunday, so I can tackle this and not feel the need to rush home." Anne loved her volunteer position at the historic Charleston hospital but also loved her newest responsibility. She and her husband, Ralph, were caring for their beautiful granddaughter while their daughter Lili was deployed. The girl was an absolute treat, and beloved, but her being at riding camp gave Anne a broader window of time to get things done, and that was nice too.

"She is the sweetest child." Shirley's voice softened.

"She is, isn't she?" Anne mellowed her voice too, because there was something special and youthful about taking on a busy seven-year-old with thoughts and ideas of her own. "She invigorates us. Me, especially, because Ralph's time here at the hospital has grown since he retired from his pastoral duties at St. Michael's."

"Horning in on his pretty wife's gig, that's what I say," Shirley teased.

"I can't disagree," Anne said. "I love that man, but sometimes a pastor's wife needs a distraction, and that's what Mercy Hospital has been for me. Volunteering here is my way of giving back, and it's given me something of my own that had nothing to do with St. Michael's. But time marches on, and my hideaway has been infiltrated by my industrious and kindhearted husband." Anne pulled a cabinet door open and sneezed three times as the dust tickled her nose. Eyes running, she groaned and snatched a handful of tissues from an equally dusty box nearby. "One of these days I'm going to hide out in this room and just dust, dust, dust. If I do that, Evelyn will happily tackle the necessary reorganization."

"And I'm steering clear of the mess," said Shirley with a slanted look toward the nearby tabletop, "but I'll be right back with your coffee, Sweetness."

Anne blotted her nose and waved her thanks.

The nickname made her smile. Shirley had dubbed her that during her first weeks on the job, and the name had struck a chord between them. Finding a fast friend wasn't an easy task, and it didn't grow easier with age, which made Anne's quick friendship with Shirley a true blessing. She stooped low and reached into the cabinet marked HISTORICAL RECORDS AND REPORTS. A thin layer of dust coated the inside of the cabinet too.

She dampened a paper towel with a spray bottle and swept it across the shelf before withdrawing a thick bundle of folders and news clippings. She set them on the table. She retrieved several more stacks from the lower shelves then paused when her hand bumped something flat and hard.

She set the folders down then crouched real low. She got so low that she blessed her daily workout routine because regular exercise was the only thing that made it possible to half crawl into the stupid cabinet to retrieve this last object.

Grasping the front corner, she nudged the object forward.

A box.

And not a regular box, not a cardboard box filled with musty papers, the unfortunate norm in many of these metal storage cabinets.

It was a wooden box, plain and old. Real old. Anne had a measure of respect for old things, but she was more a farm-chic kind of decorator, so their cozy bungalow not far from Addie's school was done in warm ivories with splashes of color. But this—

She set the box on the table then perched on one of the three stools that had been thick with dust when she walked in. She'd wiped them down first thing, and she'd just opened the box when Shirley came in with their drinks. Evelyn Perry came in behind her and lifted her brows in surprise when she spotted the box. "What's that? And what's it doing in the Vault?"

Evelyn Perry had been Anne's friend for years, and it was Evelyn who talked Anne into doing hospital volunteer work over three decades before. Evelyn was in charge of the current records room, situated between these archives and the busy ER admissions desk and waiting area. "No clue," Anne told her. She nudged the metal cabinet door shut with her foot. "It was buried in the farthest corner of this wretchedly overstuffed cabinet. Tucked so far back that if I hadn't practically crawled into the cabinet, I wouldn't have seen it." With gloved hands, she slowly raised the lid.

Anne thought the box would smell musty.

It didn't.

And with the top raised, several folded-up papers and a host of old photographs became visible. All black-and-white except three, toward the bottom. Those were in full color and not badly faded.

"Anne, I can't imagine what this is all about," said Evelyn as she and Shirley watched. "But then," she continued, "I've made it a point to stay as far away from those cabinets as I can. Something about deep dark recesses repels my good nature. Although I have pledged to do something about this room. It's out of control." Evelyn liked organization, and if it didn't exist, she'd make sure it happened. The vintage records room overhaul had made her summer short list.

"This is very interesting," said Shirley, peeking over Anne's shoulder. "Some of those pictures look to be nearly a century old, but I don't see anything to do with the hospital, then or now. Do you?" she queried the other ladies.

Evelyn slipped one of the ever-present pencils from her updo and lifted several photos with the eraser end. "Not a thing. They seem to be shots taken at a school, perhaps. This one, with these young women sitting at tables? Definitely a school setting, wouldn't you say? Even these others seem to be school related. The children playing. The old brick of that building." She pointed to a corner of the building at one side.

Shirley took a paper from the box, unfolded it, and drew a sharp breath.

"What is it, Shirl?" Anne reached out a hand.

"Looks like a treasure map," said Shirley as she handed it over. "Written on the back of an old prescription paper, so that makes it even more authentic. *X* marks the spot."

"Treasure map?" Anne accepted the paper, studied it, and then handed it to Evelyn as she and Shirley unfolded two more sheets of matching paper.

"A poem." Anne flipped the prescription paper over, revealing the first part of a verse. "'The kiss of the sun for pardon, The song of the birds for mirth—'"

"'One is nearer God's heart in a garden,'" continued Shirley from her paper. "'Than anywhere else on Earth.'"

"Oh, that's lovely," said Evelyn softly. "Despite my lack of finesse in the garden, that touches my heart. And my soul."

"It's odd to have this written on two sheets instead of one, though," mused Anne. "A game, maybe? Because all three are on the same kind of paper. Pharmaceutical paper, and nothing too recent either."

"For kids to find a treasure," declared Evelyn. She was childless, but she and her history-loving husband were beloved by a slew of other people's children. A fair share of them called Evelyn "Grandma Evie," and she loved the title. "Absolutely innovative, wouldn't you agree?"

"But who in their right mind would hide scribblings of a kids' game in a box, in the back of the lowest shelf of a cabinet that no one ever ventures into?" Shirley didn't sound convinced. "That makes no sense."

"With pictures," noted Evelyn. "The only pictures I'd expect to find in here would be of hospital functions, and if my sinuses didn't go into full meltdown over dust, I'd have this room in ship-shape order already. But"—her eyes began to water right then—"not without a good cleaning and an allergy pill. What's that you've got, Anne?" she asked as Anne held a picture aloft. She reached for a tissue but spotted the dust on the tissue box and sniffled instead.

"Romance," breathed Anne, holding the picture up for Shirley and Evelyn to see. "Look at these two. The longing in their eyes. That expression of—" She paused then stood up and moved toward the light. When she got beneath it, she extended the picture out to brighten the image. "Byron Wellington."

"Who?" Shirley asked as Evelyn moved toward Anne.

Evelyn put her reading glasses into place and looked as surprised as Anne felt. "He sure looks like Byron, but Byron is our age or a bit younger," she reminded Anne. "The man in this picture is in his late twenties or early thirties, don't you think? Byron's father, maybe? The resemblance is striking. I see it, plain as day."

"Grandfather, more likely," said Shirley as she glanced at her watch and moved toward the door connecting the records area to the archives. "He'd be at least a hundred and twenty by now, judging from the date on the back, and there aren't many men out there having babies in their sixties. Especially not back then," she added. "Duty calls. I'm off to work, ladies. See you later."

"Thanks for the latte, Shirley," Anne said. "I'm buying next time."

"And I'll let you." Shirley hurried off with a wave, and Evelyn turned back toward the pictures. "This is weird, Anne."

It was.

Not just finding a box in a recessed corner but finding a box with personal artifacts that had nothing to do with the hospital. "You see the resemblance, don't you?"

"Vividly," agreed Evelyn. "But Byron left under such awful circumstances. I can't imagine why this would be here or what it means. Or why—"

Anne lifted the last folded paper in the box, tucked beneath the photographs. These sheets were full-size and folded in thirds like an official business letter. There were three pages stapled together. As she unfolded the front-facing paper, four meaningful words jumped out at her, done in fancy type, scrolled across the top quarter of the paper. And when she read those words, she looked from the document to Evelyn and whistled softly. "Good night, nurse! It's someone's will, Evie." She pointed to the date. "1991. What on earth is it doing here?" she wondered.

Evelyn leaned over and read the will out loud. "'I, Richard Byron Wellington, do hereby bequeath the sum of three thousand dollars to each of these grandchildren: Dale Wellington, Patience Wellington Connors, Susannah Montgomery, Abel Jackson, and Adrianna Jackson Summers. The remainder of my estate and all of my physical properties and real estate are hereby bequeathed to my oldest grandson, Dr. Byron Michael Wellington, who always understood the value of education and stopped at nothing to achieve it. If bequests are not freely accepted through the law firm of Morris, Morris & Whitaker within thirty years, all rights will revert to the Greater Charleston Preservation Society to do with as they deem fit. Signed by me, this seventh day of August, in the year of our Lord 1991.'"

It was signed, *Richard Byron Wellington, Esquire.*

Two witness names were scrawled beneath Richard Wellington's signature, and the paper bore the official seal of having been accepted as a legal document—but was it still legal and binding?

Anne had no idea. "Evelyn, what do you think? Do you think Dr. Wellington ever got this? Or even knew about it? It was written about the same time he disappeared. Unless..." Anne's breath caught in her throat. "Unless someone knew about this thirty-year clause and Byron didn't just walk away." A thought that had never once crossed her mind crossed it now. "Maybe someone made him disappear."

"Murder?" Evelyn couldn't have looked more surprised if she tried. "Anne, that's impossible. And yet—" As she studied the will and then the calendar on the far wall, she took a deep breath.

"Maybe not impossible at all."

"The best time to commit a crime is when it can be most easily covered up," noted Anne. "I read that in a British mystery, and it's true. If circumstances act as a natural shroud, what better time to make things go your way?"

"Never let a good crisis go to waste," muttered Evelyn. "Although the perpetrator wouldn't have hidden this here, Anne. It wouldn't make sense, right? If you were party to a crime, you'd dispose of the evidence. Not hide it. So who did?" She tapped a finger to her mouth as she pondered.

"And why?" asked Anne.

"We've got to do something," declared Evelyn as the records bell chimed a waiting customer. "Let's talk later, okay? We'll grab Joy too, because the minute I saw that date, I got that chill straight up my back, and we know what that means."

Anne knew, all right. That chill meant they were on the right track of something. Only this time—

With Charleston's love-hate relationship for expansion, dating back a good thirty years since Lorilyn Cochran took over the preservation society and hadn't let go—

It could be murder.

Chapter Two

ANNE SETTLED INTO A SHADED chair between Shirley and Joy and across from Evelyn that afternoon. A break in the heat and humidity made sitting outside pleasant, and that wasn't always the case in a Charleston summer. They'd arranged to meet in the Grove, a parklike area nestled between the hospital wings, the parking garage, and the businesses facing Tradd Street. The garage was linked to the hospital by two walkways, one on the ground level and one on the second floor making access easier for employees, patients, and visitors. Between the recent expansions and renovations was this shaded oasis, crisscrossed by sidewalks linking buildings. The Grove was a popular spot for folks to gather until the heat and humidity drove them indoors. A short respite from the typically oppressive July heat allowed the women to talk quietly on-site. South of them, the famed and historic Angel of Mercy statue stood sentinel over what used to be a main entrance of the harbor-based hospital. A prominent path provided right and left turns to access adjacent professional buildings and treatment areas.

"He was an amazing young trauma surgeon, he had military field training, and he came to us from New York City after working there during some of their worst times in the 1980s." Anne knew that Evelyn didn't like to frown. Frowning inspired wrinkles and Evelyn wasn't a fan of wrinkles, but her sober face was enough to reflect her emotion. "He was brought in by the administrators. There was a clutch of doctors who thought they ran the show back then. Their egos got to busting buttons, so the admins coaxed Byron into the ER. They wanted to shake things up, and there were a few staffers who didn't care to be shaken."

"Dr. Schlater topped that list," noted Anne quietly. Geoff Schlater was in his early seventies now, and on one of the hospital boards. He wasn't practicing any longer, but his power-hungry nature had only grown with time. "Even then Dr. Schlater wasn't the kind of man who liked to be shown up," she added. "The director made a fuss about how good Byron was—"

"Which literally put a target on his back because inflated egos were the norm on the surgical floor and the ER," Evelyn cut in.

"Clearly a situation that hasn't changed," said Shirley, and they all knew she meant Dr. Chad Barnhardt, the ER chief. "It's lucky for Dr. Barnhardt that he's good at saving lives because that's the only thing saving him from a piece of my mind." She took a long draw on her ever-present ice water. "You don't think those doctors hurt Byron, do you?"

"Well, he disappeared after a huge malpractice suit was filed against him and the hospital for the deaths of twin boys who were brought in after a horrible crash on the interstate."

"Mercy!" Shirley's brows arched high. "Losing two children, what those parents must have gone through."

"It was unbelievably tragic," said Anne. "They were traveling through town on the interstate, heading home from vacation, so no one knew them. The boys were in the third seat, both six years old. Their little sister was in the middle seat, in a car seat. She wasn't badly injured, nor were the parents, but those boys…" She sighed softly. "It was heartbreaking."

"There was only one doctor for both boys?" asked Shirley.

"No," Anne replied. She didn't mentally revisit this time often, because the sad outcome had weighed on the entire staff. "Byron was overseeing their care with a skilled resident and the surgical team. Dr. Schlater was on the surgical team. The timing was awful because there had been a bus/truck accident and a resulting pileup on the interstate near the Air Force base. That accident triggered this collision. The ERs were overwhelmed, and the parents and the sister were sent to other hospitals. Being bigger, the Medical University of South Carolina ER was dealing with the bus collision victims. Back then the hospitals didn't drill massive trauma as much as they do now. Normally the boys would have been taken there." She turned her attention to Joy and Shirley. "MUSC was a primary trauma site back then too, but they were swamped. Everyone was beyond capacity, but that didn't change the level of care the two boys received. The damage from the high-speed rear-end collision was just too great."

"Oh, that's awful." Joy covered Anne's hand with hers.

"It was dreadful, and there was no way to contact the parents about the fate of the boys, so they came into the ER nearly three hours later to find that their boys were gone. My Ralph had come to the hospital to provide counseling to people." Anne paused, remembering the heartbreaking scene, and had to catch her breath. "Sorry, I just haven't thought about all this in a long time."

"Other pastors went to MUSC," Evelyn added. "The whole thing was such a tragedy. A beautiful day, no weather hazards involved, just human error and over seventy people affected. Seven were lost, and at least a dozen suffered life-changing injuries. But media coverage of the two boys swept the area. Questions were raised about the EMTs, the transport, the decisions, our emergency room, our staff."

"One magazine actually did a comparative study on how poor decision-making may have affected the outcome of patients. All of it led to the lawsuit against Byron," explained Anne.

"So he just up and left?" wondered Shirley. "He didn't stay and fight? How did the directors handle it?"

"They tripped over themselves to appease the situation, but that only made things worse," said Evelyn. "One of the less-injured patients heard Dr. Schlater berating Byron about his choice of treatment. They called a reporter and shared what they overheard, and that became the basis for the litigation."

"It was horrid," Anne said. "We've had awful situations since, that's the nature of a trauma center, but that one sticks out because Byron disappeared after the lawsuit was filed and no one knew where he went."

"Although I don't know how hard anyone looked, because we were all busy with our own lives," admitted Evelyn. "We were in our thirties. Anne was raising Lili and helping at St. Philip's."

"It was about five years before Ralph was asked to take over St. Michael's," Anne added. "And I guess a part of me thought Byron deserved a chance to start over. Or maybe I was just too scared to look too hard. Not scared for him, at least not then." She sighed. "I was absolutely in awe of medical staff back then. If a doctor said 'jump,' I asked 'how high?' because I was brought up to respect them. But when I saw how they treated this brilliant young man, I was taken aback. He was so nice to me. To the nurses. To Evelyn. He went out of his way to be polite and respectful. He stood out, and I think that made some of the senior staffers even angrier.

"Evelyn and I talked about it then, but it wasn't like a volunteer and a records clerk could have any effect on hospital policy," she went on. She tapped the box lightly. "This changes things. I wonder if people knew about this will thirty years ago. Richard Wellington's beautiful estate has been sitting vacant for years, but someone must be paying for upkeep, because it hasn't fallen into disrepair. So does that mean no one's claimed it? Or that Byron is just ignoring it? Why would he do that?"

"I don't know," replied Evelyn. "But look what I found online." She handed Shirley and Joy a photo she'd printed that afternoon. "This is a photo of Wellington Manor when it was Shifting Winds over a hundred years ago. It called itself a 'home for erring women.'"

Shirley snorted. "Why is it always our fault?" she asked, but it was a rhetorical question. "Was it a good place?"

Evelyn nodded. "You know I love history…," she began.

"As do I," Shirley declared. "Mama too. Starting a new job and settling in, there hasn't been much time to explore Charleston's history, but I absolutely intend to do that. Mama would love it too. She taught me to respect the past and aim high for the future."

"That sounds just like her," agreed Evelyn. "Your mom was such a blessing throughout the whole hospital. I remember many times walking down the hall and hearing her sing a hymn to one of her patients. She even took requests."

"But getting back to the box." Joy drew her brows in slightly. "First, are we wrong to have it? It's not ours."

"It's not anyone's in the hospital," Anne answered, "and I aim to hang on to it. Someone hid it there. And if we go digging around..."

"Oh, I like the sound of this already!" Shirley clapped her hands together and smiled.

"I don't want whoever put it there to move it or take it," Anne whispered for their ears only. "Evelyn always makes sure to lock the archives door when she leaves, which is good. And I took photos of everything in the box. I've learned after too many mishaps that having things recorded is a wonderful thing. I thank the Lord for my smartphone every day." She raised her phone. "This thing is like the best invention since sliced bread and the Swiss Army knife."

"Amen to that," agreed Shirley.

"I'll make sure everyone else keeps the door locked too," Evelyn assured them. "That means they'll have to get past me to get into the archives, which, by the way, are going to get the cleaning and organizing they deserve over the next few weeks. Dust or not, I'm determined because it's a shame to have things in a muddle. I don't do muddles, and those summer interns need to learn that a hospital records job isn't just sitting and waiting for a request. It's about making your area as accessible as possible. And it'll keep them busy," she added with a quick smile. "Busy interns are less trouble than bored interns. Stacia and I agree on that." Stacia was Evelyn's assistant records clerk.

"Those organizational skills make you a great puzzle solver," said Joy. "So how can we track down this missing doctor?"

"Old-fashioned legwork," said Anne. "Evelyn, can you and Shirley do some research on the Wellington estate? If you gals jump on that, then Joy and I can double-team the search for Byron."

"Glad to," said Evelyn. "My church and Shifting Winds use the same groundskeeping service, and Lorilyn has mentioned more than once that she'd do anything to get control of the manor and make it part of the preservation society tours. It really sticks in her craw that it's been sitting there, unloved, for all this time. And she seems particularly antsy lately."

The women exchanged looks. "Maybe antsy because it's about to fall into their laps?" mused Joy. "Surely they were informed of the will's content when it was originally read—if this is the same will."

"That makes her a person of interest," declared Shirley.

Evelyn looked like she was about to disagree then awareness brightened her eyes. "Shirley, you could be right. Lorilyn moved to town a few years before Byron left, and she joined the preservation society straight off because she said it made her feel more at home here. It didn't take her long to rise in the ranks, even with two kids and a part-time job. She didn't just stumble into Charleston history. She dove in. I can't imagine her having a history with Dr. Byron, but you never know." She put her sunglasses in place and stood. "I have to meet James for supper, but I'm going to do some research on the Wellington Manor and Shifting Winds."

"Me too, and I'll ask Mama about it as well," said Shirley. She stood too. "She's got a bookcase full of Southern history. Now some she likes, and some she wags a finger at, but Mama has always looked at all sides of an issue, and that hasn't changed in all my forty-three years."

"And I'll see what I can hunt up about Byron." Anne picked up the box. "Y'all don't think it's wrong to hang on to the box, do you? Until we find something out?"

"We're not stealing it. We're utilizing our resources." Ever practical, Evelyn slid her chair back under the table. "And I for one am not going to sleep right until I make sure that nothing horrid happened to Byron Wellington. I'm kicking myself for not looking into it further way back then, so I'm willing to take on anyone who thinks we shouldn't look into it now."

"Isn't Ralph's golf league on Thursday night, Anne?" asked Joy.

Anne followed her train of thought. "It is, and Addie's at camp. We could get together and compare notes. Weekdays are crazy busy at the hospital, aren't they?"

"They are," agreed Joy. "How about if we do a sandwich supper at my place? I know I'm new here, and things aren't exactly like they were in Houston." She batted her eyelashes like a true Southern belle. "But I've got time to do some research, Evelyn."

"I think that's a great idea," Evelyn said. "Thursday it is." She turned toward Shirley. "That good for you, Shirley?"

"I should get home to Mama," she said, and there was no denying the regret in her voice. "But that's all right." She paused, then offered a different solution. "Unless we change the venue to my place. Joy?"

"I would love to see your mama, so yes." Joy nodded. "But can I bring supper from the Brown Dog?" Joy had discovered the retro sandwich shop as a newcomer and loved to sing its praises. In her words, a woman living alone had little fondness for leftovers. "My treat because then no one has to fuss or bother."

"Mama will insist on making a dessert at least, because that's the way it's done, you know."

Joy matched Shirley's smile. "Same in Houston, my friend. Even if it was a pat of cold butter on day-old bread, if you came to our home, you got a seat at the table."

"Excuse me."

In unison, the four women turned.

Chad Barnhardt approached them, and he didn't look happy. Unfortunately, that had become more normal lately. He addressed Shirley directly. "Weren't you going to oversee those final transfers upstairs? That was our agreement, I believe."

Anne gave Shirley extra points for staying seated and maintaining a calm expression because she still carried a seed of that deference for doctors when they spoke to her. Old habits died hard, it seemed.

Shirley tapped her watch. "You know current status of overtime, Doctor. The front office is a bear about it, so I don't dare mess with that. I left Katie to oversee those transfers, and I know she'll do just fine."

"She's not as thorough."

Shirley must have erred on the side of accepting the implied compliment because she simply smiled up at him. "I've noticed that she's gotten better about crossing her t's and dotting her i's the past couple of months. She was new here, same as I was, but not as experienced. I'll double-check the transfers in the morning and make sure everything was done correctly."

He nodded. "I'd appreciate it." He walked off. Normally Chad held his head high—some would say too high—but today there was a slight bend to his shoulders. As if the day wore on him.

"You handle him well, Shirley," said Anne. "I know he can be a bear at times."

"Oh, Sweetness." Shirley waved Chad off as if his bad humor was of little consequence, but Anne knew how taxing he could be. "Chad isn't the first grumpy person I've dealt with in hospitals. There were plenty of bears in Atlanta, and one thing I've learned is to make sure they don't see they've riled you. Once they do, it's a never-ending battle, so I just smile and nod my way through and do a good job. Even the worst bear can't mess you over for a job well done. But I'll stand my ground with Dr. Chad, don't you worry. When push comes to shove, I can give as good as I get. I don't expect Dr. Chad would like that very much. For now, I pray for him because he isn't a happy man, and that's a fact." She glanced toward his disappearing figure as he angled down a right-hand path through the trees. "Single, good-looking, and making powerful money, and still doesn't seem satisfied. Now that's something to pray about."

"You've embarrassed me, Shirley." Evelyn admitted what Anne was thinking. "I've let him get to me and haven't given a thought to prayer, and that puts blame on me. From now on, I'm seeing the error of my ways."

"Me too," said Anne. She folded her arms. "How about we form our own little prayer society and make Chad one of our targets? 'Where two or three gather in My name—'"

"'There I am with them,'" crowed Shirley, and she reached out to give Anne a high five. "I like that idea! But if I'm going to catch my ride, I'd better get going. I don't like to keep folks waiting."

Anne tucked the box into the woven summer satchel she'd been carrying since May. This bag was always retired in late August because pink wasn't a September color, and no one could convince her otherwise. "And I better hustle to get home for Addie's call. See you gals tomorrow."

She headed up a path that led toward Tradd Street. An old friend from St. Michael's owned a pay-by-the-hour parking lot on nearby Meeting Street. He'd given Ralph and Anne a dedicated spot as a retirement gift. It might seem like an odd gift to some, but for folks on a fixed income, daily parking for both her and Ralph took a bite out of the cookie jar fund. She turned right, circling the solarium section of the new cancer wing, then hooked a left toward the lot. On wretched weather days, she'd use the covered garage, but Sam Wright's generosity was a wonderful thing. She was just shy of the turn onto the street when a loud noise snagged her attention to the right, and as soon as she turned that way, a hard pull spun her to the left and then *snap!*

The satchel was gone.

Not her purse, on her other arm, that had debit and credit cards and nearly one hundred dollars in cash.

The satchel she carried for her lunch, or a bit of knitting, and today—

The box.

Anne started a quick-for-her pursuit as a figure in nondescript gray raced off, but there was no way to catch the fleet-of-foot bandit—not in her open-toed sandals. He or she disappeared between the buildings lining Tradd, and Anne knew she'd never catch up.

She spun around again to see who or what had made the sound that pulled her attention at that moment.

No one was there. Not one soul was in that stretch of walkway with her. On one side, a plain brick wall of the cancer wing faced her. On the other, white stucco bordered the shaded walkway. No windows. No people. Nothing that could have made a sound.

So what did she hear? What snagged her attention?

And who grabbed the bag on this one particular day when it held the box of Byron Wellington's history?

Her heart didn't just beat in her chest.

It raced, and not out of fear. No, sir.

It couldn't be a coincidence that someone snatched her quarter of a ham sandwich with mustard, a just-begun quilt square, and Byron's box, which meant that her instincts were solid once again.

Something bad had happened to Byron Wellington nearly thirty years ago, and she was determined now more than ever to find out exactly what that something was.

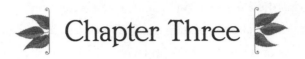 Chapter Three

"SOMEONE STOLE YOUR BAG?" EXCLAIMED Evelyn at 7:40 the next morning when Anne met her just beyond the Angel of Mercy statue. Rose-throated cream-toned hibiscus thrummed with bees and hummingbirds. Backed by a dozen blooming rose of Sharon bushes, the garden was a Monet sea of pinks and ivory, stunningly beautiful with a splash of gold and red in the rudbeckia lining the walk. The hospital gardeners had created an eye-catching effect along this part of the path, a tribute to the angel's quiet call to prayer. Evelyn grasped Anne's hand. "I couldn't believe the text you sent. James said we should call the police and I assured him that you'd done exactly that. Then I had to backtrack and say at least"—she sighed softly when she recognized Anne's expression—"I hoped you did."

"I didn't," replied Anne. She kept her voice a whisper. "I couldn't," she added softly, "because I'm not sure of our endgame yet, and until I am, I didn't want to stir up trouble for someone."

"It's not someone," Evelyn replied. There was no mistaking the worry in her tone. She took a breath and sighed. "It's a thief, Anne. A plain old thief who should be reported to authorities."

"And yet that thief didn't target my purse with money and cards and my license. He or she took the bag that only yesterday had something of note. Byron's box."

Evelyn stared at her. "You think they stole your bag because of the box? A box that was hidden for decades? A box no one knows about except us?"

"Us and whoever hid it in the cabinet," mused Anne. "Evelyn, that thief wasn't targeting my cash or my cards or my mostly eaten ham sandwich. Whoever it was had to be after the box."

"But how could anyone even know... Oh!" She smacked a hand against her forehead and stared up the walk toward the Grove. "Because we sat in the open and talked about it and even had it out for anyone to see. Clearly we're not the finely tuned sleuths we'd love to be." She groaned. "What were we thinking, Anne?"

"We wrongly assumed that no one was still around who knew anything, but Evelyn, this is a good thing," declared Anne. "Clearly there's at least one person who knows something about Byron and the box. Now we just have to figure out who it is and why they took the box."

"And where they stashed the body," whispered Evelyn hotly. "Anne, this might be over our heads, but I'm so mad that someone did that to you that I'll do whatever it takes to find the answers. No one steals things from my friend and gets away with it. Even a murderer."

"Except you could be wrong there," said Anne thoughtfully. "Whoever it is did get away with murder if Byron is dead—which I hope he isn't," she hastened to add. "What a wretched end that would be for a good, smart man. We might be researching a cold case technically, but it seemed pretty hot about sixteen hours ago, let me tell you."

"Oh, I'm sure it did." Sympathy marked Evelyn's expression. "You must have been so scared."

"A little scared at first, then surprised, then determined," Anne said cheerfully. "Until that happened, everything was supposition, Evelyn. Now we know that someone has something to hide. I'm just glad I thought to photograph everything in the box. That's a huge relief."

"Were you expecting someone to steal it?" asked Evelyn.

Anne shook her head. "No. I figured someone might force us to hand it over before our investigation is done, and I wanted to know what every scrap of paper said and who was in each photo. Then I sent each file to my email account. That way I've got them saved someplace other than my phone. After the bag-snatching incident, it seemed prudent to make sure I had additional backup."

"Anne, I never knew you had a real sleuth's heart. I'm going to guess you've been watching BritBox TV."

"Guilty as charged," laughed Anne as they moved toward the main entrance around the corner. "But you couldn't pay me to live in one of those quaint little towns where murders happen here, there, and everywhere," she went on as they turned the corner. The security guard waved them through with a quick smile. "Ralph likes crossword puzzles, but I prefer real-life puzzles. Figuring out people and their motives is a greater challenge."

Anne waved to a couple of nurses. "By the time I finished with Addie's call and making a quick supper, I had no time to do any online investigating. But Joy did, and she asked us to meet in the records room whenever Shirley has a lunch break. She said she'd leave Lacy in charge of the gift shop. I'm on patient discharge today, so I'll be all over the place." One of Anne's favorite jobs was guiding discharged patients and their families to the semicircle drive at the back of the hospital, although those moments had their share of sorrows too.

Evelyn veered off to head to the records department. "I'll text you."

"Perfect."

Anne moved toward the discharge area, situated behind the ER. The curved drive didn't sport the prettiness of the Grove or the angel garden, but it was quick and efficient. Midway through the morning, a soft and almost cheeky whistle sounded from the silver elevators as she approached them with an empty wheelchair. She laughed because she recognized that whistle. "Well, hey, handsome."

Ralph gave her a quick kiss. "It always feels so good when I see my pretty wife in her hospital volunteer smock."

"That's because you didn't have to pay for it," she teased. "No credit card bills always makes you happy."

"Agreed. How's your morning?" he asked as he pressed the button for the third floor.

"Hectic. I'll go up with you. I'm headed to three for a discharge."

"And I'm going to pray for a child who won't be going back to his earthly home," he said softly.

"Oh, Ralph."

He grimaced, and Anne knew why. They'd lost their oldest daughter to leukemia at age four. It was when Lili was a baby, and they'd felt twice robbed to say goodbye to their precious child and have to miss nearly eighteen months of Lili's life because the constant travel for Ariane's intensive treatments had been a time-drain. But Ralph's pastoral warmth and his true-life experience had shaped him into an ideal champion for families in crisis. "God has blessed you with the faith and compassion this family needs," she said as they entered the upward-bound elevator together.

"And He blessed me with you." Ralph squeezed her hand lightly. "There is mostly not a day goes by that I don't remember that, Anne. Although last week's burned hot dogs were a test," he teased.

"I may have forgotten them in my quest for a pretty garden," she said. The hot dogs had caught fire on the grill, and Anne and Ralph had taken Addie to her favorite chicken restaurant as a result. And since Anne liked chicken more than hot dogs, it wasn't a complete bust. The elevator chugged to a stop at the third floor. "I'll see you tonight." She let go of the wheelchair and squeezed Ralph's hand. "And I'll be praying for you, my beloved."

"You always do."

He returned the squeeze and headed onto the brightly decorated children's floor. Hand-painted murals of leaves and trees lined the halls. In the distance, dinosaurs roamed plains and valleys, while the closer animals were mammals and birds. At the bottom of the wall, a sea of gray, blue, and green held aquatic animals, large and small. The local artists had created murals depicting timelines and food chains in an engaging array of colors, and the administrators continued the bright spectral tones and joy throughout the floor.

She saw Ralph showing his staff card to the security person staffing the locked double doors to the unit.

There had been no locked doors when Ariane was a patient. They'd shared her treatment with MUSC and St. Jude Hospital in Tennessee. Back then the walls had been a plain cream sporting bright sprigs of flowers here and there. Fundraisers, walks, and dinners had raised the millions of dollars needed to upgrade their children's floor, and it was beautiful. Anne and Ralph had given time, talent, and treasure to help make that happen because making a terminally ill child's treatment days and final days as calm and joyful as possible was an important goal.

She turned toward the smaller anteroom holding discharge and pediatric day surgery patients.

"Anne, thank you for coming right up." A nurse wearing a bright pink set of scrubs decorated with ice cream cones waved her over. "This is our last discharge for the day," she said cheerfully as a scowling middle-aged woman helped a teenage girl stand. "Anne will take you down. I hope you feel better soon, Mariliese."

"I'm sure she will." The woman shrugged a bag onto her shoulder as Anne helped the girl get settled into the wheelchair. "We certainly could have walked to the elevator, but I suppose rules are rules."

"Exactly." The nurse gave her a commiserative nod. "We have to follow them. Oh, wait, you forgot your instructions from the doctor." She crossed to the seat Mariliese had been using and picked up the typical two-page bundle of notes. "Here you go. I've circled your follow-up appointment."

The mother's mouth thinned. She said nothing, but she took the papers with a quick move and led the way out the door. As soon as they'd turned the corner and the door clicked shut behind them, she stuffed the follow-up papers into a trash can near the elevators.

"Mom, we need that."

"We won't."

"Mom." Mariliese's voice hardened. "We will. I have to have pre-natal appointments. You know that, even if you don't want to admit it. Haven't I already apologized enough?"

The woman darted an embarrassed look at Anne.

Anne hit the button for the ground floor. Should she stay out of the conversation? Pretend invisibility? Unfortunately she'd left her cloak of invisibility at home. She waited what seemed like an interminable length of time for the elevator, then turned to the woman. "Our daughter surprised us with a baby seven years ago."

The woman instantly went stiff.

"Now she's a decorated officer in the Air Force and our granddaughter stays with us while her mom is deployed. Having Addie with us has been good therapy." The elevator slid to a stop, and the doors opened. Fortunately no one was inside at the moment. "It took a while to get over the shock. But then we realized what a blessing the baby was. It worked out."

The girl flashed a little smile Anne's way. Anne returned it.

Stone-faced, the woman said nothing.

They got to the ground floor. A man was waiting outside, standing alongside a glossy SUV. Seeing them, he moved toward the automatic doors as they exited the building. His gaze searched the woman's, and then he hurried forward and took Mariliese's hand. "Hey, beautiful. How are you feeling? Better?"

"Yes." She looked up at him and hesitated. Then she said, "They hydrated me and said I need to see a baby doctor, Dad." She paused, her expression hopeful. Clearly this was a major family surprise.

"Then that's what we'll do," he told her. As she stood up, he wrapped her in a hug that brought tears to Anne's eyes. "We've gotten through all kinds of things, Mariliese." He leaned back and smiled at her. "We'll do all right with this too."

"Oh, Daddy."

He held her then, and as Anne moved away, she prayed that the mother would be able to step out in grace and forgiveness too. Anne knew personally how important and difficult that could be, but she'd clung to the Lord's directive during hard times. *Forgive us our trespasses as we forgive those who trespass against us.*

The truth in those words had been her guide.

Her phone buzzed in her pocket.

She'd meant to grab a coffee, but there was no time now. It was time to meet the gals.

She hurried down the hall and spotted Shirley quickstepping toward the records department with an iced caramel latte.

"How did you know that there wasn't one minute of break time after 8:35?" asked Anne as she grasped the cold coffee from Shirley's hand.

"Because we were able to send thirteen patients upstairs, and that nearly cleaned out our holding area in the ER," Shirley told her. "That meant you had to be going up and down all morning, Anne."

"I was." She took a sip of the coffee and sighed, happy. "Perfect. Thank you, Shirley."

"You are most welcome, and I do believe I have some interesting things to share." Shirley lowered her voice on that last part as Evelyn's assistant took over the records desk while they all slipped into the historic and dusty archives.

Only they weren't so dusty now, and Anne turned, surprised. "Evelyn, either you dove in early today or the hospital elves have gotten busy in here."

"Elves resembling interns." Evelyn looked pleased with the day's progress. "Organization is the goal, but cleanliness was the first order of events."

"Bring on the hazmat suits," joked Joy.

"Pretty much," drawled Evelyn. "But they got a good start, didn't they? Shirley, you said you and your mom found something?"

Shirley perched a hip on one of the lower cabinets, set her water bottle alongside, and arched her left eyebrow. "That home for unwed mothers? Shifting Winds?"

The ladies nodded.

"That was some kind of place," she told them.

"Bad," whispered Joy, and she grimaced, as if she really didn't want to hear what Shirley had to say.

"No, not at all." Shirley shook her head. With Shirley, action accentuated every word. "It was given some kind of award a hundred years ago because they had just under four hundred births there and didn't lose one mother or child in the nearly thirty years they were operational."

"How can that be right?" wondered Anne. "I'm no expert, but our historic gravesites attest to the high loss of women and babies in the late nineteenth and early twentieth centuries. Do you think they fudged the records?"

"That's about fourteen births a year," noted Evelyn. "So not a lot compared to hospital standards."

"But in a home with a midwife attending. And the same midwife stayed throughout," noted Shirley. "My mama was amazed at that."

"As she should be." Anne leaned against one of the cleaned cabinets. "One midwife for three decades? That kind of dedication is almost unheard of. When did this home close?"

"World War I."

"Was Dr. Wellington called into service? To treat the troops?"

"Yes," Shirley said, "but not in the way you'd expect. Robert Wellington wasn't a medical doctor."

Three sets of eyebrows raised in unison. "What was he?" asked Anne.

"A reverend. The Most Reverend Robert Wellington of Old St. Andrew's Church upriver."

"Just down the road from the manor," said Evelyn. "I knew the family were members there, but I had no idea that one of the Wellingtons actually rectored the church. It's a beautiful Anglican church," she added in an aside to Joy. "A historic treasure, and quite welcoming."

"Mama and I decided to check it out on Sunday because their service is before ours at AME, and we wanted a legitimate look-see," continued Shirley. "An archived article Mama found refers to Reverend Wellington as a rare man who could serve both man and God. He lost his wife in childbirth. They had two young children, and it's said that he turned Wellington Manor into a house of service to women in need when he lost his wife. He stayed in the rectory across the street."

"Well, the need to care for unexpected motherhood has been around from the beginning of time," noted Joy, "but some of these places were not kindly to mothers. The judgment of people hasn't always been one of compassion. I read *The Scarlet Letter*," she added in a wry tone. "It didn't speak well of women in trouble and ministers, if you get my drift."

"The patients, or clients—" Shirley frowned, confused. "Residents, maybe? I'm not sure what we would call the mothers, but in any case, there are numerous testimonials about his kindness and his school. And about the midwife, a Mrs. Davis, who ran the place and delivered the babies and tended gardens with no help other than a kitchen cook. And the school had a teacher, of course."

"School?" The uptick in Evelyn's voice highlighted her surprise. "I heard there was a Wellington School, but I never paid much attention to it, because it's not in the historical listings of local schools. Where was it located?"

"Right there on the grounds," Shirley replied. "In a smaller building toward the back. The reverend established a school for the mothers. Not all of them were young enough to be in need, but he wanted them equipped to work and support themselves and their babies when they left."

"They took their babies?" Evelyn must have forgotten her rule about not causing wrinkles, because her eyes opened wide. "They didn't give them up for adoption?"

"Rarely," said Shirley. "That was only done in the most extreme cases. The congregation saw to it that the mothers were given whatever they needed, from diapers to groceries, as they were sent off into the communities. Some of the women were given highest recommendations to find work. The fact that many of them wrote fondly of the St. Andrew's parish and the reverend is a marvelous testimony. The only downside Mama and I could find was that it was a segregated community. There were no Black mothers allowed."

"Oh, Shirley." Joy reached a hand to Shirley's arm.

"Well that was then," Shirley declared. "Thankfully, most women of color can access good care now, if they can afford it. But looking at this, I think we need to get a look at the Wellington place, y'all."

"I agree." Joy nodded.

"How about Saturday?" asked Evelyn.

"I'm off, so I'm free," Shirley told them. "Of course, it's private property."

"It is," Evelyn agreed. "If anyone objects to us strolling the grounds, we'll handle it then. The caretakers do a nice job keeping things trim, especially around the windows. If you get my drift."

"Peeping into old, empty rooms is always a thrill, isn't it?" Joy made the remark, and a less likely image of a window peeper couldn't exist. Joy's prim and proper appearance covered a mischievous spirit. "Great shadows from those big trees early in the day," she added. "Nine o'clock?"

"Barring an emergency, yes." Anne finished her cold coffee. Her phone buzzed a text right then. She scanned it quickly and moved toward the door. "It seems we're starting to back up on floors two and five, so I'm going to head there. I'll see y'all tomorrow night. We can plan our little adventure." She hurried away and decided not to mention their Saturday trespass to her beloved husband. Ralph understood that she was the kind of person who liked to fix things in need of fixing, but he also respected protocol.

So did Anne, generally, but since there was absolutely no one to ask for permission to walk the grounds, the potential for good outweighed other aspects. Whatever happened to Byron Wellington should have been investigated long ago.

So, now?

Better late than never.

Shifting Winds Home for Erring Women

September 1890

An insistent rap on the door pulled Helen from what could have been a normal night's sleep. She pulled on her wrapper and gathered it around her middle before she answered the door. Lottie stood there, a girl in her early teens, with the awkward complexion to prove it.

"It's begun, Mrs. Davis." Fear and worry formed lines on the teen's face. "And I don't know what to do."

"Well I do, so we'll handle this just fine, Lottie." She put a reassuring hand on the teen's shoulder. The girl was only six years older than Helen's own precious daughter. "You head back to your room. I'll take Miri across the way and be right with you."

"Yes, ma'am." A contraction took hold right then. Lottie braced her hands against the wall, leaning in, and breathed in and out like she'd been taught, but the duration of the contraction pushed Helen to speed.

"Well done." She smiled brightly at the girl, and as soon as Lottie had moved toward the right-hand hall, she threw her clothes on, woke Miriam, and hustled her over to the rectory. She rapped sharply on the windowpane, the signal that meant a baby was coming. Three sharp raps. A pause. And then three more.

Robert appeared at the door quickly and opened it.

"You weren't sleeping, Reverend?"

"I saw Lottie pacing the grounds earlier, and my instincts said to stay awake longer than usual."

"And a fine instinct it was," she said. "I brought Miri to stay here while we deliver." Some nights Colleen was around when labor presented itself, but if she had gone home, the reverend kept a second bed in little Jacob's room, partially because Cora couldn't abide waking to a surprise visitor in hers.

"Her bed is ready and waiting," he assured them both. "Jacob is always excited when he wakes up to find that Miriam has come to stay over."

"Then he'll have a glorious morning." Miriam yawned and started to smile up at the reverend, but another yawn made it impossible.

"I've got her, Mrs. Davis. No fear."

"I know you do, sir." She kissed her daughter's forehead then hurried back to the beautiful home, lush with gorgeous plantings, covered walkways, and connected gardens and ponds. It was a place of peace and acceptance, made so by a man of God whose sole intention was to be the hands and feet of the Lord right here on earth, a task Robert Wellington did well.

He'd known sorrow and sin.

So had she.

But together they had made a beautiful and safe surrounding for women in their time of trial. He offered his entire estate. She offered the work of her hands and her knowledge, ensuring the safety of women and newborns.

And they offered prayer. Above all things, maybe that's what made this place stand out.

Where two or three are gathered together in My name, there am I in the midst of them.

Christ's words, made true in a home for unwed mothers. It was Helen's job to make sure it stayed that way. It was a job she didn't just treasure. It was a task meant to wipe the slate clean. She'd stay at her task for as long as that took. And that just might be forever.

Chapter Four

"This is pure pleasure." Regina Bashore sat back in her recliner on Thursday evening. She didn't have to smile and sigh to show her satisfaction, but she did both anyway. "To have such fine company, and all from the hospital I love. Sweet magnolias in bloom, Mercy Hospital was good to me," she went on, and it was easy to see where Shirley got her lyrical voice from. "It provided a good living, especially the last twenty years I was there, and I learned so much. So much." She sighed again as if caught in some sweet memory, then drew a breath. "Of course there weren't a lot of people of color working in professional positions when I started. Black doctors seemed to mostly go north, and Black nurses were few and far between down here, but my mother was a stickler for education, you know."

"She busted a lot of buttons bragging on her girl, I remember that quite well," said Shirley.

"And did the same for her granddaughter." Regina's smile grew as she regarded Shirley. "My mother knew folks and they knew her, and she used to talk about Reverend Wellington now and again, but that story was old in her time, so I never gave a real firm listen, you know?"

"There are so many things I wish I'd taken notes or listened better when my mother was alive," confessed Joy. "I could kick myself now."

"You don't remember anything, Mama?" asked Shirley. She was slicing an icebox cake Regina had made for them, and the sweet scent of lemon filled the air like a breath of summer.

"I remember his children both did quite well, and they spread their good fortune around in a most generous way. During troubled times they donated funds and supplies to good causes. The hospital at MUSC was a favorite of the son's while the daughter shared her wealth with several schools. They had a love for helping others and such a respect for learning, but they weren't very successful at teaching their own children the value of hard work or sharing the wealth. By the time they got to your generation"—she indicated the ladies with a jut of her chin—"some were ambitious, but others waited for life to hand them this, that, and the other thing, and that only gets you so far. I'd forgotten all about the older Dr. Wellington's will until Shirley reminded me, but oh!" She made her eyes go wide. "What a kabobble there was over that, let me tell you. I don't think that will was forty-eight hours old before lawsuits were filed against the grandson that inherited the estate."

"Lawsuits?" Evelyn nodded when Shirley looked at her, knife poised over the cake, but when Shirley handed her a piece on a plate, Evelyn just sighed and handed it back. "Double that, please, I have no willpower when it comes to icebox cake. Or anything else cold and delicious this time of year. So people sued the estate?" She posed the question to Regina, and the elderly woman nodded.

"They did, and I don't know how it all came out, but I'm pretty sure the will held tight, for all the good it did because the doctor grandson—"

"Byron."

She bobbed her head to Anne. "Yes, him, he never claimed the estate, and that made things worse for a bit, but then people do as people do, and time went on, and the grand house has just sat there, lonely as could be, waiting for someone to make it a home again. It survived times of tempest and a time when folks went to burn it, all mad and riled up about something or other, but that was a hundred years back, so nothing to do with what all y'all are lookin' into."

"Burn the manor?" Evelyn asked, shocked. "Who would do such a thing?"

Regina shrugged. "I don't know. It was never said."

Anne made a note to check the lawsuits. Had they all failed? Clearly no one else was handed the manor.

But who filed the suits? And what did they stand to gain?

"Regina, this lemon cake is divine." Joy waggled her fork in the air. "I've never had better."

"Rosemary," Regina told her. "Mama taught me to put tiny bits of fresh rosemary in the lemon cookies. You get a full-on dose of the lemon in the cookie and the filling, but the rosemary in the cookies makes this cake like no other."

"I can't disagree," said Evelyn. "It's marvelous. And Regina, thank you for the information you've shared," she added as she stood. "Your insights are invaluable."

"You are most welcome!" The praise made Regina's dark brown eyes sparkle. "It feels good to be puzzling things out and thinking things through. I think half the problem with old brains isn't so much the brains going wackadoodle. It's the sitting and not doing. I was saying that very thing today when that chorus girl came by with all her skirts and baubles and bangles dancing with her every move."

Shirley had been laying a thin sheet of plastic wrap over the remaining cake, but Regina's words brought her attention around swiftly. "A chorus girl, Mama?" Anne assumed her easy expression was meant to humor her mother. Regina's declining memory tended to combine old and new with abandon on her bad days, but she'd been right on top of things tonight.

"I was just that surprised," declared Regina. "There I was, settin' and rockin' on the porch, enjoying my fifteen minutes of fresh air." She added an aside to the other ladies. "That's all the heat and humidity these old bones can abide, I'll tell you, but the chilled air tends to make bones ache, so I divvy things up."

"So should we all," Evelyn told her. Her kind words deepened Regina's smile.

"But Mama, a chorus girl?" Shirley made a face of disbelief. "This town has its share of characters, but I've yet to see a chorus girl going door-to-door."

"If you'd been home midday you'd have been an eyewitness," Regina told her in a no-nonsense voice. "Not too young, and not so old, but the makeup makes a difference there, of course, so she could have been most any age, I suppose."

Shirley slipped onto a hammock near her mother's feet. "Is this for real, Mama? Or maybe something you saw a while back?"

Regina straightened her shoulders. "I think I know when I see something and when I don't, Shirley Mae. She was just as real as you and me and came waltzing up the walk, quick as can be, wondering if I might be related to you, to which I replied 'Yes, ma'am! That's my daughter, a nurse, just like her mama, and a fine one to boot.'"

"She asked about Shirley?" said Anne.

"She asked about me?" asked Shirley at the very same moment.

"That's what I said, and when I told her you were my daughter, she said I should be proud of all the hard work you're doing at the hospital and that she's certain with all that they've got you doing in the ER, you won't have time for messin' about in other people's business, which was an odd thing to say, wasn't it?"

A shiver snaked its way down Anne's back.

Evelyn's gaze went firm. "Was she issuing a warning, Regina?"

"I don't rightly know, but now that you mention it, maybe?" Regina's face went still. "At the time I just thought it an odd thing to say. She didn't stay. She tried to drop off a pamphlet that I wouldn't be reading, so I handed it right back."

"A pamphlet, Mama?" Shirley kept her voice calm, but Anne didn't miss the effort it took.

"One of those glossy ones, Shirley, but you know I'm content at the church I've been attendin' for decades. And I've never had a chorus girl come dancin' up the walk to hand out church talk, that's for sure. An odd thing, for certain."

"It would have been under other circumstances, but after having my bag snatched within hours of finding the box, I'm pretty sure it's not the last peculiar thing we're going to encounter." Anne exchanged looks with Shirley, Joy, and Evelyn. "Regina, do you remember what this chorus girl looked like?"

"She looked like all of those made-up gals in a New York City show, the ones that stand behind everyone else. Where they do all the same moves."

"A chorus girl."

"That's what I said, Shirley Mae. And this one had a real flowy skirt and all kinds of scarves and bangles and bracelets and one of those—what do you call it—a peasant blouse? And she had another scarf on her head. She parked her car by the Jacksons' place, and I caught that it was blue or gray or silver up the way, but if you were watching her, you didn't have time to notice a vehicle. Do you think she was trouble?" The sparkle in Regina's eyes dimmed. "I didn't think much of it, being summer and street actors doing this, that, and the other thing, although we don't have them here. The waterfront, yes. But not here."

"It's fine, Mama."

Anne took the cue from Shirley and patted Regina's arm. "There are all sorts that come out when the weather sweetens, aren't there? And I do believe those flowy skirts are far more comfy when the air hangs like a thick, wet curtain than some of the slacks and leggings we seem determined to wear." She stood and slung her purse over her shoulder. "Thank you for hosting us tonight, Regina. It was absolutely delightful."

She started moving toward the door and the other ladies followed, offering their thanks.

"Mama, I'll see the ladies out, and then we'll have just enough time to see *Jeopardy!* if you've a mind."

"I'd like that, Shirley." Regina seemed to have forgotten all about her chorus girl encounter. "I've got my water and my eight o'clock pills. I'm all set."

When they got to the porch, Evelyn turned. "Wouldn't someone have noticed a woman dressed like that walking around?" she whispered. "Do you feel odd asking your neighbors?"

"I will once Mama's settled. You think it was a real person?" Shirley's expression mixed concern with disbelief. "Why would someone come meandering up the walk asking about my work? It doesn't—" She paused. Swallowed. And pointed to the porch pillar ahead of them. Shrouded from anyone coming in, the note was clear and concise for anyone coming out the door. STOP YOUR SNOOPING NOW AND NO ONE GETS HURT. BEWARE.

Evelyn's mouth dropped open. So did Joy's. They both turned toward Shirley. Her mouth was agape right up until she marched across the porch, snatched the note from its pushpin, and whirled back to her friends. "First the bag and now a threatening note, and if that doesn't scream unsolved crime then nothing does. Ladies." She handed Anne the note and folded her arms across her chest. "Whatever we do and whatever it takes, we are going to figure this out, because no one"—her narrowed gaze punctuated the tone and words—"gets to threaten me, my mama, or my friends. One way or another, we will find this 'chorus girl,' and I guarantee she won't be doin' some high-kickin' Rockettes dance when we do."

# Chapter Five

RALPH WAS SITTING IN HIS favorite recliner when Anne slipped into the house a quarter hour later. He was engrossed in a self-help book he didn't need, but that was Ralph's way, always trying to improve himself and the world around him. After nearly forty years of marriage, she liked him just fine the way he was. She hung her purse on a hook inside the nearby closet and moved his way. "Husband, dear, we have to talk."

His pretended expression of fear made her smile.

"Ralph. I'm serious."

"I see that, darlin', and that's what strikes fear into the heart of every normal man, when his woman utters those four words. But we've got the house to ourselves, so what's going on?" He set the book and his reading glasses aside, and while she explained everything that had happened, he listened carefully. Then he held up his hand. "This sounds like a dicey business, Anne."

"It sounds like monkey business," she retorted.

"True, but I'd prefer to keep my beautiful wife in one piece," he reminded her. "Not just because I love her, but there's a kid who's eventually coming home from camp. She likes regular meals, and you know I'm not a cook. Therefore, keeping you in one piece is in my best interests."

"Oh, Ralph." She laughed, and he made room for her in the wide recliner and patted the seat. And then he snuggled her close and kissed the top of her head. "I love you, Ralph Mabry."

"I know you do, and I return the sentiment. But I also know I'm not going to be able to talk you out of pursuing answers on whatever happened to that young doctor, correct?"

"One hundred percent, because we should have done it long ago. I'm just making up for lost time."

"Could this chorus girl person have been the same one who stole your bag yesterday?"

Anne drew her brows down. "I don't know. The person certainly wasn't dressed as Regina described."

"Could you tell if it was a man or a woman?"

"No. Just fast. And in good shape. Lean."

"So maybe people working together?"

"Or people hired to work together."

"By who?" He tipped his head down to catch her gaze. "Who would do that?"

"A murderer who fears getting caught after running free for thirty years?"

His look of concern deepened. "Anne, people kill for less than that."

"And maybe already did," she reminded him.

"Exactly why we have a police department, my love. They're trained to do these things. That's why they have detectives. Don't they look into cold cases all the time?"

"But there is no cold case, Ralph." She sat forward, turned, and faced him. He'd just nailed the problem. "There's a disappearance that wasn't looked into, there were malpractice lawsuits, and there's the box that's now been taken."

"Did you save your photos of the sheets and pictures to a cloud?"

"I sure did, even though they automatically go to the phone's cloud. I've got them, and they're safe."

"But how would someone even know you'd found the box? What would that likelihood be?" He frowned. "Someone who happened to hide a box away in a rarely used cabinet stumbles across you and the box for the thirty minutes or so that you gals are in the Grove and puts it all together? That's way too coincidental."

Anne stared at him. Then she kissed him, full on, right on the mouth before she jumped up. "That's it! You did it!"

"I did? Well, go me."

She laughed at his puzzled look, took him by the hands, and pulled him up, out of the chair. "There was a whole group of people around when Aurora went off on her little tirade about aspersions to our old medical records and poor medical care. They all heard her order me to leave no part of the Vault unsearched to find whatever I could to wipe that image clean. 'Empty every corner if you have to,' she said. Someone in that crowd must have known I might find the box."

"Was it a big group of people?" he wondered.

She grimaced. "Sizable. A lot of folks coming in to work and some leaving, not too many visitors because it was early, and anyone working at the information desk. But who could it have been?"

"Darlin', they didn't just *remodel* the lobby when they did those major renovations a few years back. They updated the security, so everyone who was in that lobby at that time should be on the security tape."

He was right. No security system was foolproof, but the upgrades should help. Anne pulled out her phone and texted the other women. Three firm thumbs-ups meant they agreed. Whoever it was had probably witnessed Aurora's meltdown, which meant they knew that Anne was involved and had deduced that Shirley was involved as well. And if that person watched them meet in the Grove—

And Anne was pretty sure they must have been watching, because her bag was snatched on the way out—

They would have pegged Evelyn and Joy too.

Evelyn texted back a quick message. FOUR AGAINST ONE, ANNE. ODDS IN OUR FAVOR!

Two more thumbs-ups appeared before Anne turned off the phone for the night.

Four against one.

Good odds, as Evelyn noted, but who was their adversary? And who was on that surveillance tape?

That would be her first move the next morning, to scout out security and look at that tape, and if they didn't want her to see it, she'd go up to Garrison Baker's office and have him approve the request. As a hospital administrator, Garrison wanted Mercy Hospital run like a well-oiled machine. He also wanted the hospital's heart to beat for the good of humankind. Two goals that were sometimes at odds. But if anyone could do it, Garrison could.

Not all the staff liked him, but Anne and Ralph did. He shared their vision that a place didn't have to be bigger to rank among the best, and that money wasn't always the answer. Faith, hope, and charity were better cornerstones.

Anne pulled into her parking spot facing Meeting Street a little after seven on Friday morning. Shirley's shift was early, and she'd agreed to meet Anne and go to the security office together. It was tucked into an out-of-the-way alcove to the left of the main entrance, in the back of the remodeled historic wing. Anne rapped on the door as Shirley approached from the opposite direction. "I'm glad they've reopened those side doors," she told Anne as she inched her carryall bag higher on her shoulder. "Walking around half the complex was probably good for my heart health but tough on my feet. Which only means I should be walking more. I told Mama that and all she did was laugh at me. That's the problem with folks who are naturally thin," she went on. "Mama can eat a bag of chips and lose weight, but if I don't measure every ounce and gram of this and that, I'm headed toward the broad-sized side of the closet. Good morning, Anne."

Anne laughed and knocked on the door again. "Shirley, you look beautiful, and I think you're in great shape, but I was glad when they reopened those entrances too. It's nice to be able to access areas of the complex without having to go up a floor, cross over, and come back down." She was about to say more when the security office door opened.

"Yes?" A well-dressed man faced them. Youngish. Midthirties. Handsome in that rugged undercover cop kind of way. He tapped his watch. "You ladies are early today." He pointed to Anne. "I have you on the schedule at eight, and Nurse Bashore at seven thirty."

"You have everyone's schedule?" Anne hadn't thought of that. "Even volunteers?"

"If there's a problem, we need to know who's expected to be where, any time of the day. Visitors and deliveries add to the confusion, but we keep track best we can. How can I help you?"

"Anne's bag was stolen as she was leaving the Grove two days ago," Shirley told him. "Yanked right off her shoulder."

The man frowned. "Did you report it?" Then he seemed to realize where they were, and he opened the door wider. "Come in, ladies. Let's make this private."

Anne gave a glance around, but there was no one in sight, which meant they probably weren't being followed 24/7.

Yet.

She followed Shirley into the office. It was small but then branched into a larger space with a cache of screens facing two directions. Two chairs, each facing an array of monitors, sat in front of consoles with a laptop-styled setup, an array of digital "knobs," and a microphone that went to the public-address system. "Wow."

He smiled. "It's not perfect, but it's a step up from what we had when I started here. The Gaylord Foundation slipped us some funds last month after the angel statue went missing."

"I knew he funded the updates, but I had no idea they were this good. I'm impressed." Anne whistled softly. "Do you keep the tapes of each day?"

He nodded. "Digitally. Not hard copy. But we don't tape the entire Grove," he told her apologetically. "Where was your bag stolen?"

"The green space at the far end of the cancer wing before it opens onto Tradd Street," she said. "But that's not what I was hoping to see."

He lifted both brows. "No?"

"That morning I was given some very loud directions by an irate person, and I think they were overheard by the person who stole my bag."

Now his brows drew in and down. "I don't get it."

There was a pause, and then Shirley said, "We think the person who overheard the direction knew Anne might discover something they didn't want discovered."

"And did you?" he asked Anne. When she didn't answer, he folded his arms and sighed. "Whether you did or didn't isn't the current question, but if you did discover something, it was clearly hospital property. So did you take hospital property out of the building, Anne? Because that could be a chargeable offense. And I apologize, I never introduced myself. I'm Seamus McCord, head of hospital security. The quiet guy, behind the scenes."

Shirley's mouth had dropped open at his insinuation about Anne. She folded her arms, mimicking his stance, and lifted one of her dark, well-shaped brows and scowled. "First off, Anne did not take hospital anything out of that nasty old cave of a room, and don't you think for one minute she did."

"Ms. Bashore—"

"Uh!" Shirley held up her hand, palm out, and it was clear she meant business. "She found something that belongs to a friend who has nothing to do with the hospital anymore. She wants to make sure it's returned to him, so she took it to give to him. There's no rule against that, is there?"

He didn't look convinced, but he didn't look combative either, so that was good.

"Can we see the footage?" Anne asked. "To see who was in the lobby area at the time? Someone who overheard that conversation knew about what we found. If I could just see it..."

He shook his head but looked regretful. "I can't show you without administrative permission. If you can get Mr. Baker to sign off on it—"

"I totally understand." She exchanged a look of agreement with Shirley before shifting her attention back to Seamus McCord. "We'll stop up there this morning," Anne told him. She couldn't be angry at this young man. The sincerity of his intent to do a good job meant a great deal to the safety and sanctity of Mercy Hospital. "Thank you for looking out for all of us at Mercy. I know it's not an easy job."

He smiled then, and something in that smile touched her. She was pretty sure that Seamus didn't always get the thanks he and his staff deserved. He followed them to the door and opened it for them. "I'm here until three thirty today. Have Mr. Baker email or text me permission, and I'll have that recording ready to pull up. It's a busy time of day and we have multiple feeds coming in from the lobby, so you'll see a lot. Maybe you'll get lucky and recognize someone."

Anne gave him a bright smile. "It's the reactions I look for. Who turns? Who doesn't turn but stands quiet, listening? Who pretends to be hunting for something in her purse so she can hear a little more? Linger longer?"

"A detective mindset," Seamus noted with a grin.

"A youth group leader on campouts," she corrected him and laughed. "Almost the same thing. And an avid mystery buff."

His smile said he understood. After he closed the door, she and Shirley hurried toward their respective assignments. Shirley had just enough time to cross the lobby and descend the wide, sloping hallway that led to the red elevators and the ER wing beyond them. Anne had plenty of time, so she walked with her. "I'll call Garrison's office. If you can get away for ten minutes between eleven and one, maybe we can snag ten minutes of his lunch."

"He lunches at his desk?"

"Almost every day," said Anne. "He's determined to keep things running smoothly. Seamlessly smooth, he calls it. Like the good Lord's tunic."

"He said that?" Something in Shirley's voice made Anne look at her more closely.

She nodded. "He surely did, and it was a poet's moment, I'll tell you. Who'd have thought that from a big, burly guy like Garrison?"

"It's not something I've noticed in other administrators, that's for sure," said Shirley. She gave Anne a quick hug. "I suspected a kindly heart in that man the moment I met him. Nice to see my suspicions were correct. See you later." She hurried off, and Anne moved back to the lobby. She greeted the gals already staffing the information desk then went to stand where she'd been two mornings before, when Aurora had pitched her little fit. She created a quick sketch of where she was in relation to the three camera angles she'd recognized as she watched the monitors beyond Seamus's office. A building filled with sick people, drugs, and emotion could lend itself to confrontations. More than once she'd thanked God for the swift response of Mercy Hospital's security team. She signed in and began her shift at the front desk.

Most administrators didn't come through this way. They preferred slipping in the discharge door and taking the silver elevators up to the fifth floor, but Garrison had been different from the beginning. He liked to see and be seen. He wasn't effusive. Ralph referred to him as quietly cordial. It was an apt description, but when he didn't come through the lobby, she took a quick detour when Aurora asked her to oversee discharge duty later that morning.

She enjoyed this task, and numerous others around the hospital she'd called home for nearly three decades. She slipped down the hall to the administrative wing of Five, their shortened name for the fifth floor, and hurried up to the administrative assistant's desk. "Julie, can you get me ten minutes with Garrison sometime today? I have a security request for him, and you know I wouldn't ask if it wasn't important."

"He's tight today, Anne." Julie had gone to school with Lili, and she'd attended St. Michael's for years until she and her husband moved to James Island. She was frowning as she perused the screen before her when Garrison approached the desk.

"Good morning, Anne."

Anne turned his way. Garrison's cultured voice would have been perfect for commercial voice-overs. "Garrison, good morning to you."

"Julie, what's going on?" He asked the question in an easy tone, but Anne knew the strength behind the mild demeanor.

"Anne needs a short time with you, and you have no time. None."

Garrison shifted his attention to Anne. "I'd fit you in now, but I expect you're up here to escort a patient out, correct?"

"Yes."

He didn't pull out a phone to glance at his daily calendar. Anne was pretty sure Garrison came to work with his daily appointments memorized. "Can you break free at twelve forty-five?"

"Lunchtime," scolded Julie, but she smiled up at him. "Watch it, or you're going to become even more loved than you already are. Except you're showing up others, Garrison, and that's rarely a good thing." She swept the bank of offices a quick look, then arched a brow.

"To each his own," he returned mildly. "Does that work for you, Anne?"

"Perfectly. And thank you so much. It will be brief, I promise."

He laughed softly, a round, rolling laugh. "Don't make promises you can't keep, and if you don't mind me eating my sack of PB&Js while we talk, we can stretch it to fifteen minutes."

She had to respect a major hospital administrator who sat at his desk and ate peanut butter and jelly sandwiches. Which meant she should give him a jar of her homemade preserves. "Thank you, Garrison." She hurried back past the bank of elevators to escort the patient downstairs per hospital regulations. If all went well, she should be seeing that recorded confrontation in a few hours. And that should be interesting.

Chapter Six

SHIRLEY MET ANNE JUST OUTSIDE the silver elevators at twelve forty. "I've got thirty minutes. I switched up lunchtime with Kitty and Katie, and—mercy!—I trip over my tongue every time I call for one of them. No two people who look so much alike should have such similar names."

"It's funny, isn't it?" said Anne as the elevator slid to a stop in front of them. "You'd think they were sisters, but they're not, just two great nurses who happen to look alike and have alliterative names."

"It's embarrassing that I have to look at their name tags every now and again to make sure I'm talking to the right one," Shirley confessed when they'd stepped into the elevator and the doors slid closed with a quiet hum. "I don't have problems with names, but that pair of doppelgängers confounds me now and again. Mr. Baker knows we're coming?"

Anne flinched inwardly because she hadn't thought to mention Shirley to Garrison. Out loud she said, "I told him I'd be brief and wouldn't mind if he ate his peanut butter and jelly sandwiches while we talked."

Shirley laughed, and when they got to Garrison's office, he looked up—

Saw them—

And Anne was sure his eyes lit up when he spotted Shirley. He stood, rounded the desk, and welcomed them in, then he closed the door firmly before he turned. He moved back to his desk and smiled at Shirley. "Nurse Bashore, I want to thank you again for the invite to Mother Emmanuel church. I went to the later service the past two weeks and found the pastor to be enlightening and inspirational. Maybe this week I'll come to the early service and maybe run into you and your mother?"

"Most often, yes, although we're visiting Old St. Andrew's this weekend because of some puzzling things in Charleston's past. Mama and I do like to ferret out information as needed."

"Then the following week? The nine o'clock service? And if there's time, I'd enjoy some visiting time with you and your mother afterward. I find that Sundays in a new city tend to stretch long, and it's months before football season kicks off."

"Only if you call me Shirley," she said in her typical firm voice, but her eyes danced as she said it. She reached into her bag and removed a jar of homemade strawberry jam and handed it to him with a smile. "I know we talked about your love of peanut butter and jelly sandwiches a few weeks back, and I kept meaning to get a jar of our strawberry preserves to you. Mama and I made this back in May. We freeze the berries first. I find it gives them a better chance to release their juice in the cooking, and Mama says you won't find better jam anywhere."

The humble gift seemed to delight him. "Thank you." He held the jar up and met Shirley's gaze. "It's much appreciated."

"You are most welcome. I didn't bring it to bribe you into seeing our way on this matter of Anne's, but I am not opposed to that. Just so you know."

"Warning noted. So what can I do for you ladies?"

Anne explained what had happened over the last seventy-two hours, and while Garrison lifted a brow when she confessed to putting the box into her bag, he actually congratulated her on having the presence of mind to photograph the contents, page by page, before she left the hospital. His sandwich sat waiting while he folded his hands and leaned across the desk. "You ladies are aware that safety is a key issue in hospitals these days. Maybe not so much in small rural settings, but in cities that seem to well up with unrest now and again, it's become imperative to have good security systems in place. But that doesn't mean we want to invade others' privacy or spy on them."

"Of course not." Anne stayed practical. "That would be an abuse of power. This is different, because I was the inadvertent receiver of a very loud dressing down in a public area that put me at risk." She didn't stress her point, but then, with Garrison, she wouldn't have to. "I think Aurora's unhinged moment put me in danger, and it could also be putting someone else in danger. If, in fact, Dr. Wellington is still alive. And if he isn't, then we may have a very nervous fugitive running free in this hospital. And none of us like to imagine what a dangerous person who has already killed once can do."

Garrison pulled out his phone and tapped a message, then set it down. "I've given Seamus permission to let you women see the footage. Don't copy it."

Both women shook their heads. "That thought never crossed my mind, although it's a good one," voiced Shirley. "Fortunately, we're just looking for reactions to Ms. Kingston's theatrics or an absolute nonreaction to them."

"Keep me informed?"

Anne breathed a sigh of relief. "We'd like that, Garrison. I don't want to bring trouble to this place," she said. "I've loved Mercy Hospital from the moment I walked through the doors of the ER with a sick baby girl over thirty years ago. We lost our daughter, but I gained a love and respect for medicine and the people who make it work. But on the other hand, I've seen the downside of medicine too, how egos and competitiveness get in the way. When I was younger I kept quiet. I'm different now."

"Me too," agreed Shirley.

"And right is right," continued Anne. "We need to know what happened to Byron Wellington."

Garrison stood. So did Anne and Shirley. He raised the pint jar filled with rosy red jam and dipped his chin. "This will be on tomorrow's lunch menu."

Shirley's dimples flashed. "I'm glad. That will please Mama too. She loved to feed a crowd in her day, and she misses that busyness. I've a mind to take her across the way to TriCounty Ministries. Mama likes to have her hands working, and it looks like the folks there keep body and soul together for a fair number."

"I expect they'd love the help, Shirley." Anne turned back to Garrison. "Thank you. We'll get out of your hair so you can enjoy your somewhat stale sandwich."

Garrison waved her off. "I didn't grow up on soft bread and thick jam, so a little heartiness to the bread isn't a big deal. Eating like this every day reminds me of what my mama and daddy did to keep things together. My grandma made the best soft-crusted bread I've ever had the pleasure to eat, but that recipe seemed to die with her. Or maybe the time to do a baking of bread when folks were working hard to pay bills changed things. Either way, this is a treat."

By the time Anne and Shirley met up with Evelyn and Joy at the security office, it was time for Seamus to call it a day, but he clocked out and stayed on his own time. He sent the other surveillance staff out of the area. When Shirley asked about that, he shrugged. "I'm a big believer in need-to-know. I expect you ladies aren't shrieking this all over Mercy Hospital, correct?"

"No." Joy looked almost alarmed that he would think they might. "We want justice. Not battle. But we're prepared for whatever comes our way."

He bit back a smile but not before Anne saw it and liked him all the better for minding his tongue. They might seem like a simple group of slightly-beyond-middle-aged women, but age wasn't as important as determination, and this crew had that firmly in hand.

He rolled the footage once through, and Anne watched carefully. Then she had him roll it again, only this time she stopped him repeatedly. "There." She pointed to Dr. Schlater, who had stopped in his tracks across the beautifully appointed lobby. He'd looked at Aurora, then Anne, then Aurora again, but then he dipped his chin and hurried on with an aggravated expression. Since that was Dr. Schlater's typical look, Anne wasn't sure if it meant anything or not, but he had stopped dead, and that put him on the list.

"Oh, Anne, there." Evelyn stepped forward. "The woman pushing a food cart of donuts and pastries toward the café. She's not looking at you, but she's slowed down, and you can tell she's listening."

"I wouldn't have noticed that," said Shirley. "But that may be because I had my eyes on the trays of pastries. Do those all come from our bakery in food services?"

"No, a local bakery ships in the doughnuts, bagels, and pastries," Evelyn replied. "Our staff takes them to the coffee shop, the kiosks, the cafeteria, and the sidewalk cart."

"Who is she?"

The trim woman was wearing a face mask like so many workers did when handling food, but Anne wasn't sure who it was until she spotted the leggings. Fun, flighty images of dragonflies peppered the black fabric. "Tula Manchester."

"Tula?" Evelyn frowned, then quickly smoothed her brow. "She's been gone for years."

"She was gone," Anne replied, "but she's been back for almost a year, just long enough to have her seniority in food services reinstated. She's been working the cancer center kiosk, and she's always got the cutest clothes. I duck through there on bad weather days."

"She's always been a 'notice me' kind of personality." Evelyn didn't sound very approving. "Are those dragonflies?"

"They are and mercy, they're cute!" said Shirley. "But she is definitely listening to you two. And there, see her turn?" As Tula moved forward, she steered the treat-laden cart around a pillar but then darted a look back over her shoulder toward Aurora and Anne. Although her mouth was shrouded in a decorated face mask that matched her leggings, there was no denying the flash of interest.

And then she hurried on.

When they ran through the minute-long segment of tape, Anne frowned. "Just those two? Out of all those people?"

"Well, there were a lot of curious looks but no other valid reactions," said Shirley. "Maybe that's good. We can focus our attention on these two. If I remember correctly, the not-so-good doctor was already on the short list."

Seamus turned the footage off and faced them. "First, no one is to get hurt. Do you understand me?"

His tone meant business, which only endeared him more to Anne because he was right. Safety first.

"Agreed." Evelyn shrugged. "Hopefully, there's no reason for people to go to extremes."

"And yet I am sure you ladies are determined to see this through," said Seamus.

"Well, yes." Evelyn sent him an apologetic look that really didn't have an apology attached. "We need to figure this out, and if folks are going to dash around the hospital stealing bags—"

"And if chorus girls are going to leave warning notes on old ladies' porches," said Shirley.

"Then they must be found out," Joy finished. "That's the crux of it."

Her friends were right, decided Anne as she hurried back downstairs to answer a call to the front desk.

And no matter what happened next, they would find answers. Byron deserved nothing less. She escorted a pair of elderly visitors to the newborn nursery unit in the Birthing Center. From where they'd parked, the pair had gotten hopelessly lost, so she was happy to guide them to their newest great-grandson. Then she texted the ladies, LET'S PARK AT THE OLD CHURCH AND WALK UP THE ROAD. WE WON'T BE IN ANYONE'S WAY.

Three agreement emojis sprang up like March tulips, and as she hurried home, she mulled over the two people of interest on that surveillance footage, Dr. Schlater and Tula.

The first might have every reason to disrupt their investigation, but why would Tula care?

Anne had no idea, but she planned to find out. Tula had worked in the hospital for a long time, and service employees and volunteers had a skill set few others matched in a hospital setting. They could hide in plain sight. No one much noticed them with the flurry of scrubs running this way and that.

But what could Tula possibly know about something that happened thirty years ago?

That was a question that needed answering.

Shifting Winds Home for Erring Women

September 1894

A part of me cannot bear the thought of being separated from my beloved child, my sweet Miriam, but I am caught in vexation. She is of an age now where questions flow like raindrops down rooftops, and while we've talked of things in part, to be surrounded by the sins of men and some of women can't be in her best interests, I fear.

What else can I do but send her to a boarding school? And yet my heart will be torn from my chest to do this thing, and how will I ever know a moment's peace with her gone?

I cannot.

I know this. I admit this. I am not a smothering sort of woman, but she is my only child, the only flesh of my flesh that will ever be, and it is my job to protect her from harm. If we send her to secondary school in town she could become a target of harsh tongues. To live in a house of unwed women will spur children's admonishments and Lord—

Sweet Lord!

You know that I don't want her to bear shame for my mission here.

And yet what can I do? How can I protect her?

A soft knock on her door made Helen set her pen aside. She tucked the book beneath the mattress with the others. Five books now, all filled, some with her thoughts, some with her records of birthings, solutions, and outcomes.

She moved to the door and opened it. One of the middle-life parish women stood there, a lovely woman with a gentle heart, Clara O'Herlihy. "Helen, the reverend was wondering if you could meet with us. He has some ideas for the committee to consider."

Helen was often consulted when the parish committee discussed anything connected with Shifting Winds. "Of course, Clara. I'll come right over." While Robert was the owner of the impressive home and grounds, he was also rector of the church that sat diagonally up the road, a church that had suffered severe damage in the great earthquake some eight years before a spate of hurricanes roared repeatedly along the Atlantic coast.

Weather, shrugged some.

Armageddon! insisted others.

Repairs to Shifting Winds had been minimal. A well-built structure was meant to withstand the wind's wrath, but others had suffered, and the committee was understandably careful in how it looked at disbursing funds.

She took her short cape. A warm rain was blanketing the area, leaving hot spots for breeding mosquitoes, but summer was drawing to a close. Cooler months awaited them. She and Clara went into the rectory through the kitchen. Maisy, the honey-skinned cook who had been enslaved on a nearby plantation as a child, welcomed them. "Well, if it ain't two of my favorite ladies. Miss Clara and Miss Davis, go right on in, won't you? And Miss Clara, you know you gals can come to the front door?" She tsked softly with a hint of humor. "You be front door company now, Miss Clara."

Clara laughed and hugged the older woman unabashedly. "And miss my hug from you, Maisy? I think not. Back doors suited me as a child, and they do just as well now. How's the family?" she went on. "How are the grandkids?"

Maisy's face turned plaintive. "Most are well, but we do have a situation with Augustina." She darted a look at Helen, an expression that needed no words. Maisy's youngest daughter was a headstrong young woman of seventeen.

"Maisy." Helen moved forward and spoke softly. "You know I'll help in any way I can."

"She does not listen, that one," fumed Maisy. "Her daddy and I have tried every which way to make her see the glory and goodness of God, but she is boneheaded when it comes to listening. I will be needing your services, Miss Davis. In about five months' time, the heart of winter, but Lord willing, we'll deliver a healthy child, and maybe this will grow that girl up. If only she could be more like her big sisters." Maisy had four daughters. The first three were hardworking, God-fearing young women, but Tina was cut from a different cloth, it seemed.

"I'll be available as needed," Helen assured her. She set her hands on Maisy's shoulders. "It will be all right."

"I pray so." Maisy had arranged a delicious-looking plate of wafer cookies, cheese, and crackers. "I may have overly indulged her as a girl, her being so tiny and coming so early that she needed lots of care."

Helen hadn't known that fact. "Maisy, if that baby shows signs of coming early, you send for me right off, all right?"

"Yes'm."

Would she call straightaway?

Helen wasn't sure. Maisy had a servant's heart. She wasn't one to normally ask for help, so Helen moved closer. "Maisy, you did fine with Tina's birth, in part because you were an experienced mother by then. You'd had three babies. Being young and immature makes her case more fractious."

Maisy stood still for a moment. Then she dipped her head in acknowledgment. "I hear you, Miss Davis. And I'll send for you right off. If my waitin' cost my daughter's or grandchild's life, I'd never be able to forgive myself." She raised smoky gray-brown eyes to Helen. "Thank you."

"It is truly my pleasure." She touched Maisy's arm lightly, then followed Clara to the front room.

Robert stood when they entered. He looked serious, but he'd had that appearance for years now. Too serious, in Helen's opinion. How she wished he could feel the peace of the Lord as she did, but that was between him and his

Maker. He softened his expression, waved her to a vacant chair, and then took his customary seat to the left of the small hearth. A woodstove filled the hearth space now, big enough to heat the rectory. Helen was pretty sure that previous rectors spent some mighty cold winters with nothing but that small hearth and pans of coals carried upstairs to provide warmth. She smoothed her skirt, folded her hands, and waited.

"Clara, thank you for bringing Mrs. Davis over." His gaze swept the group, and he rubbed his thumb and forefinger along his jaw, an old habit. "I've been mulling our situation here since the last hurricane thought to linger, and I've realized two things. First, that our congregation has been put upon to do repair after repair, so I've decided to sign over a sum of five thousand dollars to seed a new account for church and grounds repair."

"Sir, so much?" Ben Knowles's brows shot up. "That's a grand sum, and I fear such a move may leave you in sorry straits in years to come."

"Family investments do me well," Robert replied in a mild tone. He and his brother had invested in multiple properties over the years, and while Robert was an absentee landlord in many ways, his property manager was a wise, older man who looked at opportunity as a way to shelter the future and had done remarkably well. Helen guessed that Ben Knowles was unaware of some of this because Robert maintained degrees of separation between his family legacy and his pastoral calling.

"I confess to having an alternative interest for this meeting," he went on. "I have put this to prayer multiple times, and I have examined every side of the issue. I come to you not for permission, because this endeavor will be on my private grounds, but for understanding and prayer. I'd like to start a school."

Several puzzled expressions met his, but Helen's heart fairly jumped in her chest.

"A secondary school," he explained, and Helen didn't dare meet his eye, because what a blessing that would be.

"I thought to convert that smallish building I have on the off-side of the manor house. The one set back in the thicket of trees. It will need refurbishing, of course, and Ben, I was hoping to hire your son to do that."

"I'll have him come see you," Ben replied, and the uptick in his voice showed his pleasure. A paying job was always a welcome thing.

"It came to me during these repeated storms and the fuss over children missing lessons that the younger women at the manor suffer a similar lot. The combination of their delicate condition and lying-in keeps them away from studies for too great a time. In the drudge of winter, the days can be somewhat monotonous, so if there were an educational institution on the premises, we could continue the women's education and be a better help to them in their job search."

"That's a mighty generous thought, Robert." Melinda Hayes pressed her lips together, something she did often.

She didn't condemn Shifting Winds out loud, but she didn't offer any pretense of acceptance either. Fortunately there were only a few in Robert's congregation who felt as she did. "When you're already being such a benefactor to women who come here in undesirable circumstances."

Helen's breath caught in her chest. She had to work to keep her hands from fisting.

"It occurs to me that a hand up always outweighs a handout, Mrs. Hayes." Robert leveled a firm look her way. "What better hand up than an increased opportunity for education? Mrs. Davis, I would like your advice in the hiring of a teacher, and of course, your advice as well, Clara. You've taught your share of children—"

"And raised three so far, so yes, I'd be happy to help, Reverend Wellington."

"Good. I am open to advice and concerns, of course."

Melinda Hayes looked about to burst, but Robert nodded toward Ben first. "Ben?"

"I'd like to hear the curriculum list before the church gives its approval," he said. "While I know our approval isn't required, I'm sure it's welcome."

"Quite welcome," replied Robert. "No such list exists at the moment, but we can develop it forthwith, can't we?" He arched a brow of expectation toward Clara and Helen, and they nodded in unison.

"I would say a basis in classics with some trade work alongside," suggested Helen.

He sent her a pleased look. "A practical idea."

"And I have just the person who can teach trades," said Clara. "Elizabeth Cottorone. She runs the dress shop and millinery for her mother and brother. She's got an eye for what works and what doesn't, and her plain talk shares it readily."

"She'd be an asset for sure, if she's available a day or two per week."

"I'll ask," offered Clara.

"And if you remember," added Helen, "Delancey Delacroix was with us several years ago, and she was a teacher at the Montgomery Day Academy."

"Prior to having an illegitimate child." Melinda aimed a tiresome look at Helen. Helen had never been quite sure if Melinda didn't like her or the home, or just plain didn't like anything.

"Fortunately the Lord's promise was to forgive our trespasses as we forgive those who trespass against us," she answered firmly.

"And society's disdain is enough of a punishment, isn't it?" Robert put the thought in with folded hands. "If Miss Delancey is available, and if you ladies find her credentials suitable, I think the lesson of a woman who worked hard to garner an education and then apply it despite a change in circumstances would set the right kind of example."

It was clear that Melinda didn't agree, but Helen wasn't going to fret over that.

A school! Here, at Shifting Winds. She didn't dare speak to Robert now, for her delight was far too strong to seem selflessly motivated. If they had a school on the grounds, Miri wouldn't have to go away nor bear the insults of less kindhearted children.

Miri could stay here. Right here. Right where she belonged.

Chapter Seven

"EVELYN'S RUNNING LATE," SHIRLEY TOLD Anne and Joy the next morning after they parked their cars at the church and started walking toward the manor. "They lost power and she overslept, and you know she doesn't go anywhere without her morning exercise routine."

"It keeps her limber," said Joy. "I tried yoga once. I fell over. I've avoided it ever since. My walking routine is as radical as I care to get."

"And it's working, girlfriend." Shirley smiled at her. "Like Mama says, it pays to pay attention to little things because then they don't grow out of control. But she also says don't sweat the small stuff, so there's some contradiction there."

Anne laughed. "I found myself doing the same thing as a parent and now a grandparent. It seems my advice has become quite fluid as I've gained experience. Holy sweet magnolias, what have we here?" she said as they approached the turnoff that led to the Wellington manor. "A gate?"

It was a massive gate, strong and stern, black wrought iron, and there was nothing finely tooled or decorative about it. This gate meant business.

"Who put this up?" wondered Shirley.

"And when?" asked Joy. "You can see it's newly constructed, because the concrete footers are white."

Joy was right. The clean new concrete base hadn't been in place long. "How can we get in?" asked Anne.

Evelyn came jogging their way just then. "Sorry I'm late." She rolled her eyes at the gate, then hooked a thumb. "Follow me." She led the way back down the sidewalk, around a curve, and then darted through a gap between two thinning privet hedge bushes. The others followed, and Anne found herself in a broad, back garden area. The grand house stood to their left. Stone paths worked their way through a maze of small and not-so-small gardens. Most were grass and weeds now, mowed on a regular basis, but the walkways delineated them.

Joy's groan made the others turn her way. "I'm gonna find whoever installed that gate and let them have what for," she declared woefully. "Burrs. Hundreds of them."

"Oh, Joy." Evelyn was the first to reach her side. "We'll help." The three women began picking hundreds of tiny burdock spurs from her leggings and the back of her shirt. While the other ladies' clothes had a few of the pesky clinging seeds, Joy's pants were covered, and it was a full five minutes before they had her de-burred. "I'm so sorry that happened," Anne told her.

"The perils of being the shortest of the group?" Joy said. She was clearly more comfortable without the burrs. "But I will find the person who blocked our way, mark my words. And yes, I know it's private property and I'm trespassing, but that's neither here nor there." Her Texas accent only added weight to the statement. "My disaffiliation with burdocks goes back to a childhood moment when

I tumbled off of a small rise into a huge cluster of the dratted things, and by the time my dad was able to get to me, I was covered and scratched from stem to stern. I've killed many a burdock and thistle in my time, and this only gives me more reason to continue my vigilante approach."

Evelyn grinned. "You are clearly David to the burdock Goliath, my friend. Which way shall we go?"

"Every way," said Anne. "Let's split up and reconnect here. We can text each other what we see. That keeps things nice and quiet."

Evelyn motioned to Joy. "Come with me. I'll be on the lookout for burrs."

"And Shirley and I will go this way." Anne led the way to the left. She spotted a slip of paper that the wind and rain seemed to have plastered to the concrete side of a small pillar. She peeled it off and held it up to the light, but the cloudy morning wasn't much help. "D-a-l-e," she read, then frowned. "It goes blank there, washed out, but then there's something else ending in p-i-n-g."

"Landscaping, maybe?" guessed Shirley. "You sure it's p-i-n-g?"

"One hundred percent certain," Anne told her. She handed the paper to Shirley who, after studying it for a moment, slipped it into her waistband. "The problem with leggings is lack of pockets, for real. We might be able to discern more when it dries."

"Good thought." Anne moved along the west-side shadows of the house, then frowned. "The windows are too high."

"Common for back then," noted Shirley. "It's like that with a lot of big Southern homes unless they're on flatland. That height and a five-step approach must have made it hard for people who had mobility issues."

"But it's a stellar look, isn't it?"

"It puts the *M* in manor," said Shirley, and her dry tone made Anne grin.

She stopped grinning when she spotted footprints in a patch of mud. Footprints that led directly to a thick piece of tree stump set right beneath a window.

Footprints that weren't completely dry.

She motioned Shirley over. "Someone's here."

Shirley raised her brows. "Someone that's not us?"

Anne nodded. "Look."

Shirley came up alongside her. She studied the footprints, then the house, then pointed. "That window is unlatched."

Adrenaline buzzed through Anne when she followed the direction of Shirley's finger. The old-fashioned twist-and-turn window latch was neither twisted nor turned. "It sure is."

"So are they in there?" Shirley voiced the words in such a matter-of-fact tone that Anne's heart calmed measurably. "And if so, who are they? A transient, down on his or her luck? A homeless person? A murderer, plotting our demise at this very moment? Or maybe it's the elusive Dr. Wellington himself. That would solve our mystery right there, wouldn't it?"

The thought of the brilliant doctor holed up in a big empty house all these years made Anne sad. "Do you think it's him?" she whispered. "There are only thirty-two days left to claim his inheritance," she reminded Shirley.

"One way to find out." Shirley crossed to the window with a no-nonsense stride and drew it up. "Halloo?" she called out in her best Southern drawl. "Come right out here and show your identification, please. And don't dillydally, I have *not* got all day."

It wouldn't work. It couldn't. No one would listen to a trespassing woman and follow those directions, would they?

And yet a man who seemed to be in his fifties came their way, and he didn't look like a serial killer.

"Now, sugar, if you have a weapon of some sort, I'd advise you not to use it, because we're investigating a possible crime or series of crimes right here, and I want to hope that you aren't involved," she told him in a voice firm enough to do a drill sergeant proud. "Come on out here and tell us who you are and what you're doing in this house."

"You mean my house?" the man replied in a grumpy tone. "Maybe I should be asking you the questions, lady."

Anne studied the man carefully. Was this Dr. Wellington? Thirty years older?

Thirty very rough years older, added her brain.

She watched him as he clambered out of the window. And she watched his hands for weapons. Just in case. She absolutely refused to think about Ralph's opinion on their investigation at this moment, because she knew what he'd say, but he hadn't worked with Byron. He wasn't bearing the weight of guilt for saying nothing when a good man was maligned.

"Who are you women?"

Nope. Not Byron, she decided as he straightened his shoulders.

A man could change physically in a lot of ways, but Byron wasn't a tall man. He'd been about five foot six or seven and this man was an easy five foot ten.

"Who you are is the question right now," Anne informed him. "I know this is not your house, and you aren't Dr. Byron Wellington. His inheritance has gone unclaimed for thirty years, so who are you? And why are you here?"

He stared at her, then started walking away.

"Hey!" Anne started after him, but Shirley caught her arm.

"We have to be sensible, Sweetness, and chasing down a man caught in a place he didn't and doesn't belong isn't one bit sensible. Let's let him go but take full advantage of the opportunity he provided to us." Shirley looked left. "Open window, anyone?"

"Of course." Anne texted the others and moved forward. "It's not breaking and entering if we don't have to break anything, correct?"

"It's just entering," agreed Shirley with a grin, but that grin faded when her feet hit the floor. "How many creepy crawlies and little beasties and things that go bump in the night do you expect call this place home after being empty for so long?"

"Saints alive, I have no idea, but let's use our phone flashlights to brighten things up, okay? No one will notice them in the daylight."

Evelyn and Joy joined them a few minutes later. Joy had managed to attract more burrs, but nothing like her first encounter, and as they trained their lights around the house, Evelyn sighed. "I can see why Lorilyn has been hankering after this place for so long. It's lovely. Even if it is old and abandoned, it's inviting." She paused and looked around. "And dusted. Notice that I'm not sneezing? So that guy you found here, do you think he dusts?"

Shirley frowned. "I think we can safely assume that's a negative."

"Then who?" asked Joy as she moved into a broad side room with a large central table. "This was probably a dining room at one time." She pointed at the floor. "Those scuff marks are from chairs, but they're not bad, so maybe this had a carpet at one point."

"And that space on the wall, slightly off-color." Evelyn shined her light high at the far end of the table. "A picture gone."

"Do you think anyone else is here?" asked Joy in a soft voice. "Because I don't plan on runnin' into someone with a gun, y'all."

"I don't think so," Anne said. "It feels empty but not as lonely as I would have thought."

"A lonely house?" Joy looked around, then nodded. "You're right. Being dusted and swept up helps. I don't see any animal droppings. And no evidence of water leaks." She indicated the ceiling.

When they moved into the next room, Evelyn gasped. "I think someone is harvesting bits and pieces of this house for their own good."

Anne followed her gaze. "The tin tiles that used to be behind the stove and line this wall. They were in the online photos."

"Gone," Shirley breathed.

"I can't believe it." Anne traced a finger along the wall. "Who's doing this?"

"I don't know who, but the why is an easy answer," said Evelyn. "The tin tile place at the market sells these things for some big bucks. Folks use them to accent their homes."

A flash of lightning interrupted their musings. The crack of thunder was slow to follow, and the women exchanged looks. "Do we dare take time to go upstairs?" asked Anne.

"We have to." Joy shrugged off the storm. "We're here, that window might be locked next time, and if we let a little thunder and lightning rattle us off the trail, we'll never find the answers to this mystery."

"When she's right, she's right," said Shirley. "But let's hurry. I'll take pictures as we go, but don't let me miss anything."

"This place is huge. You are going to miss things, but let's make the most of it." Joy led the way upstairs. Now that there were no burdocks involved, her take-no-prisoners attitude shone through. "This hallway is stunning. Nowadays you can't imagine giving over this much square footage to a hall, but it adds a grandeur all its own, doesn't it?"

"It does." Anne took some pictures also while they went from bedroom to bedroom. The hallway had five bedrooms surrounding it, then two other doors. One led to a seventies-style bathroom that seemed totally out of place with everything around it, and the other was a locked door. Maybe the staircase leading to a third-floor attic?

In any case they had enough to explore with the open doors.

Two rooms held an early twentieth-century appeal. The others had been modernized, but the generous wood moldings and trim work still spoke to an earlier time.

Lightning crackled again, and this time the thunder wasn't far behind. Anne moved toward the hall. "That's our cue, ladies."

"It is. Although I hate to leave." Shirley slipped her phone back into her pocket and led the way downstairs. She crossed the two broad front rooms and got to the window first.

Lightning crackled again, cloud to cloud and cloud to ground, lighting the world around them as the dark storm flew their way on a branch-bending southwest wind.

"Do we stay and ride out the storm here? Or go?" asked Evelyn.

Anne was about to vote "stay" when another lightning bolt struck the tree beside the privet hedge.

One minute the tree was there.

The next it was on the hedge, bringing down wires and limbs in a horrible tangle of live electricity, which meant the city crews and police would be here soon. They might not take kindly to the four trespassers on private property.

"Go!" said Anne. She slipped out the window and dropped to the wet ground below. Joy, Evelyn, and Shirley followed suit. Shirley put the window back as they found it, tucked into the frame but not locked, and they all raced across the back of the manor's acreage.

The storm raged around them.

Cold, hard rain pelted Anne, and then it was rain and hail, a dreadful mix and awful for hair, as if the July humidity wasn't contentious enough.

She found a narrow gap between the bushes on the far side of the property and paused with the others on the sidewalk as sirens and flashing lights careened up and down nearby roads.

The church lay a quarter mile away, up the road and around the corner, and by the time they got to their cars, Anne was drenched, pelted, and more than a little drained. But as they jumped into their cars and started the engines, Anne knew that there would be plenty to talk about once they were all clean and dry again.

Starting with who was the guy living in Byron's house, and was he the one selling off pieces of artistic beauty? Or were there others involved? And what did all of this have to do with Byron's disappearance?

She didn't know, but as she drove back to her cozy, new-to-her home in North Charleston, Anne had every intention of finding out.

But first she'd have to figure out how to stay in touch with the other ladies when their schedules sometimes thwarted them. Texting was great, but she'd already had her bag stolen. What if someone stole their phones and could open them?

All their thoughts would be revealed.

And how could they gather at the hospital when they knew someone was already watching them there?

Chapter Eight

THE WOMEN NEEDED TO SET up a Zoom meeting.

Anne sent the text to Joy, Shirley, and Evelyn on Sunday afternoon. Ralph was doing a late-day prayer service at the hospital, and she had an unusual stretch of hours to think about the Wellington mystery. Her mind was as blank as a chalkboard in July, though, so she reached out to the other ladies. YOU IN? she texted, and two thumbs-up emojis appeared within seconds. Joy and Shirley were available.

She sent all three women a link and when Shirley and Joy had joined the meeting, Anne raised her phone so they could see the picture of one of the old prescription papers that had been in the box. "We need to figure these out."

Shirley frowned. "They're from long before your doctor friend was on the planet, right?"

"Right," Anne said, "but there's a reason they're in the box, isn't there? Whose prescription pad was it? I've found out that it's nothing they used in Charleston back then. So where did they use this particular pad?" She sent the photo to both of them, and Joy took charge.

"I can track this down," she said. "I have more time than you two right now, so let me take this part on. And Anne, I want to go see this Cochran woman. I want to meet her. There's a lot of historical information in all this, and I've got every intention of exploring Charleston history as time allows. The preservation society is a great place to begin. Can we go see her tomorrow, after work?"

"That's a great idea," Anne agreed. "Call her and set it up, Joy. You're working until three and I'm done at two tomorrow, so I'll see what I can find out in that extra hour. There are some older hospital staff who might have something to say. I'll check it out and meet you in the lobby at three. And if the subject of Wellington Manor happens to come up while we're talking to Lorilyn, we can see what her reaction is. Try as I might, I can't find a connection between her and Byron Wellington. Nothing fits."

"That's often the way when a puzzle first comes out of the box, isn't it?" mused Shirley. She tapped a finger to her jaw.

Regina walked by the screen then, and leaned in. "Hey, girls!" She waved to them, and Anne and Joy laughed as they returned the gesture.

"Hey back," called Anne.

"That is one saucy dress, Miss Regina," declared Joy, and she whistled lightly. "You look lovely."

"If a body's able to dress up for Sunday, she should do so," Regina said. "Now, Shirley is in casual attire, but I like to spend a good share of the day in my Sunday-go-to-meetin' clothes. It adds some polish to the day, don't you think?"

"And if you get taken out to supper, all the better." Joy laughed. "You're ready to rock and roll."

"With my hat." Regina set a bright green hat on her gray hair. The angled headpiece had a feather, a bow, and just the right tilt to set off her sparkling brown eyes. And the green in the hat matched the lime green in the floral dress.

"The hat makes it," Joy agreed. "I love a good hat, Miss Regina."

"As do I. It completes things. I often think that's part of why we all flock to watch British shows," Regina continued. "They know how to complete an ensemble."

"Mama, I can't disagree, you do look smart when you step out the door," said Shirley. She'd leaned back so that Regina would be seen through the small camera eye at the top of the screen.

"And a solid appearance puts the frosting on the cake," Regina replied. "I'm off to the porch for my fifteen minutes. Goodbye, girls!"

"Oh, she is darling," said Anne once she heard the click of the front door. "Shirley, I'm so glad her memory problems aren't bad yet. Maybe they never will be. She's sharp as a tack, that one."

"I think she's doing better now that we're together," Shirley said. "She's definitely perked up since I moved down here, and that made all the changing worth the while. Mama sacrificed daily for us kids. And I can't deny that I'm falling in love with this city. I'd forgotten how quaint it is after spending so many years in Atlanta." She leaned forward. "Now, if you two are tackling Lorilyn, I'm going to track down who ordered that new gate. I've got that slip of paper all dried out, and there's a clue there, someplace. The grounds are obviously being taken care of, and someone must be paying for that, yet there's nothing in that will about a trust fund for upkeep."

"Unless that was already in a trust and needed no designation," suggested Anne.

"I'll see what I can discover," Shirley said. "I'm covering the evening shift for Katie on Friday. She's in a wedding and needed the night free. Which means I'll be dog-tired Saturday. Y'all know what Friday nights are like in the ER."

Anne knew, all right. "Ralph gets called out regularly on Friday nights. And this heat puts tempers on edge."

"Heat, hot heads, and trigger fingers don't mix," Shirley declared, "but we've got a good crew at Mercy, and the worst traumas generally go to MUSC. Still, we get our share. Gotta go, I'm taking Mama to evening prayer and supper. She knows if she stays dressed up I can't resist taking her out. I want to have good times with her while I can."

Joy sighed. "Wise thinking, Shirley. I still miss my mama and my husband every single day. I'm doing fine, and being cash-comfortable is a big plus, but you never get too old to miss those you love. And that's the truth of it."

"That's so true, Joy," said Anne. "I know we'll all be reunited in God's time, but there are days when I'm on the children's floor and the what-ifs hit hard. What would Ariane's life be like now? Would she be married? With children? And then I put a lockdown on my heart because I can't let it swamp me, and it could some days, even after all this time. Then I see how far they've come with childhood leukemia, and I realize that science hasn't forgotten my loss. Nor has the good Lord." Anne smiled. "Shirley," she said, "thanks for jumping on that scrap of paper."

"Who knows, it may have flown in from a drive-by garbage truck, but I'm going to follow through and see what I can find out. See y'all tomorrow!" She left the meeting.

"Anne, this was a good idea," Joy said. "If our schedules don't allow us get-together time, this is the perfect way to touch base. And now, being inspired by Regina's classic look, I am going hat shopping down by the waterfront. Someone once said that petite women should not wear big hats. I'm about to prove them wrong. See you in the morning." She left the meeting too, and Anne was tempted to throw time to the wind and join Joy on her hat search. But she couldn't get Byron's image out of her mind. He'd been real. Earnest. Hardworking. Brilliant. They'd let him slip away like sands in an hourglass, and while she hadn't been a friend of his, she'd admired the man.

Ralph came in a little later. He set two fried chicken takeout dinners on the counter, and her smile inspired his grin. "I figured cooking wasn't making the short list, and Sundays and fried chicken seem to go together."

"Oh, you are so right," she said, giving him a big hug. "And Ralph, I think I found something. Something odd. I was searching for all of Byron's relatives online—"

"Internet stalking."

"Basically." She grinned up at him, and he laughed. "Anyway, I found most of the people mentioned in the grandfather's will. It's interesting that he skipped an entire generation in his bequests, isn't it? But anyway, there's this fellow." She pulled up a picture of a young man with a brazen grin, hamming it up for the camera. He was standing with two other men of a similar age.

"I'm assuming this picture was before he was cut out of the will?"

"That's not him." She pointed to the caption below. "This is Byron, this is his cousin Abel Jackson, and this is Joe Brown."

"Now there's an alias if I ever heard one," said Ralph as he unwrapped the dinners.

"Except it's not. He was listed in Abel's wedding announcement. I miss wedding announcements," she added. "That was always my favorite part of a daily paper. The babies and the weddings. Anyway, Joe is still in this area. He's got an address in an apartment complex upriver, but I'm pretty sure he's the man we ran into in the Wellington house yesterday."

Ralph stopped withdrawing chicken. "You were on the grounds of an abandoned old house? That's what you ladies were off doing?"

"Of course." She didn't have to pretend her surprise. "Ralph, if we're going to solve this missing person affair, we have to look, don't we? And where better to explore than the manor in question? But that's not the point. The point is what would this Joe Brown—"

"Aka possible ax murderer," muttered Ralph.

"He seemed harmless enough," she insisted, "but I did resist following him to find out more information, just in case."

Ralph ran a hand across his jaw. "Anne, I—"

"Here's the amazing part," she went on. "In his will, Richard Wellington implied that he gave Byron the bulk of his estate because Byron went on to higher education. Apparently the others must not have. But Abel Jackson isn't a no-education nobody like his grandpa seemed to think. He invented the software that allows internet tracking of people's shopping habits and then interfaced it with all major platforms. He's worth more than a quarter billion and has homes all over, including one here, on the waterfront. But back then"—she pointed to the picture—"when the will was made public, he got into a terrible fight with Byron. It made the papers. They arrested Abel and this guy Joe and let Byron go free, because they didn't believe a trauma surgeon would risk his hands in a fistfight."

"You think his cousin went after him to finish the task?" asked Ralph, and he wasn't sighing now. He was listening intently. "You think this millionaire might have killed his cousin out of jealousy?"

"I don't know. But I can understand if he was upset about the will. What if he did it, Ralph?"

"A guy with that kind of money and clout probably wouldn't hesitate to use either or both to throw a quartet of middle-aged women off the scent, Anne. Or kill them," he added. "This can't go on, honey. It's dangerous."

"It isn't if it's not him," she argued as she unwrapped her own dinner and sighed with happiness. The fragrance of crisply fried chicken was one of her favorites. "He may have nothing to do with any of this, but it's something to check out, isn't it?"

Ralph's eyebrows couldn't have gone higher. "No. It's something to leave to the experts."

"Ralph. Darling." Anne leaned over and planted a feather-light kiss to his cheek. "There is only one way to become good at things, and that's to do them. You know I'm good at reading people, and there's not much I'm afraid of."

"More's the pity." He spoke under his breath, but he was listening.

"You help people every day, and some of them aren't very nice people," she reminded him. "I don't argue with that, I don't caution you away, because you're so good at it. Oddly, darling, I'm good at following rabbit trails. A good person doesn't turn their back on the chance to make the world a better place. You know that's true," she added pertly when he started to frown. "Are you saying grace? Or should I do it tonight?"

Ralph said grace, but it wasn't in his normal easy tone. His voice held a tinge of worry, and when he asked God to cover Anne and the ladies with a veil of protection, she squeezed his hand.

Ralph was old school enough to want to protect his wife, but he also knew his wife. Anne wasn't one to stand for injustice, and if she could fix this old wrong with some good friends, she aimed to do it.

Chapter Nine

ANNE WAS WAITING AT THE Angel of Mercy statue at two fifteen when Fanny Edison came into work the next afternoon. She'd arranged the meeting because Fanny was a surgical nurse when Byron was on staff thirty years before. Now Fanny worked per diem, enough to keep her busy but have her weekends off when she wanted them and time to spoil her grandbabies. She spotted Anne and hurried her way.

"Gracious, woman, it's hot and humid out here, isn't it? Sure you don't want to have this little meet-and-greet indoors?" Fanny swept a tissue to her brow. "I came in on the bus. You can't beat that senior pricing. Even if I were to find free parking on an evening shift, the wear and tear on my car is way more than that dollar deal we get. Now that's a good use of taxes." She moved toward a shaded area to the left of the angel. "What's going on, Anne?"

Anne explained her interest in Byron and the thirty-year limited endowment, but she didn't mention the box or anything else. She wasn't going to lie to Fanny, but she didn't have to reveal every detail either. "So I'm wondering if you recall something I don't," she said. "Something that might get me on the right track, because if something happened to him I want to make sure he's informed. I was a new volunteer back then," she added, "so I wasn't traveling in trauma surgeon circles. But Dr. Wellington was a good man, and if I can make this better, I will."

"Oh, you did bring this up at a most interesting time, Anne." Fanny clucked her tongue. "I was just thinking about Byron the other day when I saw a recap on that horrible accident on cable news. I don't know why they think they have to rehash that whole thing—it was bad enough living it—but I can tell you that Byron Wellington did nothing wrong. Not one thing. If anyone in Charleston could have saved those boys, it was him, and Dr. Schlater hung him out to dry on purpose. He is an ego-driven man, and he's got no power over me now," Fanny sat up straighter. "Back then he was my boss, and he made life tough for so many. A single mother earning a solid living doesn't rock the boat, especially in a city as pricey as this one. But as for Byron leaving, little Tula Manchester might have better information on that. They had a thing, you know."

Anne most certainly did not know. "A thing? Like a romance?"

"Oh, yes, it was a sweet thing for certain," she cooed. "Like a Cinderella story come to life. The kitchen help and the great surgeon, but when everything fell apart—"

"She left him high and dry," Anne supposed, but Fanny shook her head.

"No, ma'am, it was the other way around. He left her and broke her heart, and then he just kind of disappeared. I swear that woman loves him still. She does the Spirits of Magnolia Cemetery ghost tours at night, did you know that?"

Anne shook her head. "I've never been on a ghost tour. I was always thinking that someone from the congregation would see me there and call me out for it. Although I love the historical aspects of them."

"Well, Tula loves to play a role. She's done community theater, but this pays pretty well and it's only for six months a year. And when she moans and mourns for the spectators, land sakes, you'd think she was the real deal. If there were any such thing, which there is not," she finished on a long breath.

"Of course not," Anne agreed, and had to bite back her excitement.

Tula and Byron?

Tula was in the lobby when Aurora was issuing the loud order to find old records in the vintage records room.

Tula could have been the chorus girl.

And—

The more Anne considered it—

She could have been the fleet-of-foot bandit. Tula wasn't a typical fiftysomething. Anne had seen her dance in community theater presentations. Tula could move. Could this all be related to one prime suspect? A woman scorned?

She thanked Fanny and went inside to meet Joy. Joy still had a quarter hour left until quitting time, so Anne took a seat in the lobby and let the cool air bathe her while she did a search on her phone. When the ghost tour options populated the screen, she chose the one Fanny mentioned, then scrolled for Tula's name. Her tour was listed as sold out for that night, but there were two spots left for Tuesday evening.

Anne wasn't sure who would be able to go with her, but she booked the two tickets right away. Seeing Tula in passing in the hospital was one thing. Seeing her in action on a ghost tour was quite another, and Anne wanted to get a real look at the woman who might be part of the shadows surrounding Byron's disappearance.

Either way, she sure hoped no one from St. Michael's would be there.

"Oh. Anne. I didn't know you were joining us." Lorilyn didn't look upset to see Anne, but there was no hiding the look of surprise on her face. Clearly she thought she was seeing Joy on her own.

"Anne and I have become good friends since I arrived in Charleston," Joy explained. "Our granddaughters are close in age, so we have a lot in common. Shall we grab a drink at Ginger's?"

When Lorilyn looked confused, Joy amended her offer. "The East Bay Café. I've gotten used to calling it Ginger's because she certainly has a presence, doesn't she? I know Bud and Ginger run it together, but it's Ginger's persona, through and through. And it's a wise man who knows when to step back and let his woman run with the ball."

"Absolutely." Lorilyn turned to head toward the popular coffee shop. "They're open until seven, which is nice too."

"That's something our snowbirds find disturbing about the South," Joy said. "So many of our coffee shops have the nerve to close midafternoon. That means they're forced to go to chain coffee shops, which doesn't sit well with them, let me tell you. I hear about it in the gift shop all the time. Still, there are few options after three o'clock, so when I got to Ginger's place I knew I was home, sweet home."

"We Southerners do like our traditions," said Lorilyn.

Anne stayed purposefully silent. This was Joy's appointment, and her conversation. Anne was simply here as an observer. Once they had their iced coffees, they settled into a quiet corner of the coffee shop. For a café that was frantically busy in the morning and just normally busy midday, the late afternoon was more moderate. A bunch of filled tables but nothing overwhelming. Lorilyn slipped her small purse off her shoulder and looped it over the seat back. "When did you move to town, Joy?"

"Not too long ago. My daughter and son-in-law are here with my precious granddaughters. My son-in-law is a civilian contractor with the Joint Base, so it's not a job he can do from just any old place. When I lost my husband, I wanted to be near them. I loved my roses in Houston but not nearly as much as I love my daughter, so I sold off the Atkins homestead and headed east. I actually have roots here—my Gillespie and Stinson ancestors came to Charleston with the Reverend Martin back in the seventeen hundreds as part of the Scotch-Irish immigration."

Lorilyn's eyes went wide. "Are you serious? That was a landmark immigration—not only for here, but it set the stage for later immigrants from Ireland who were suffering from money-grubbing landlords and failed crops."

"Well, the Reverend Martin seems to have been a real force in his time. I think my Scotch-Irish heritage has given me a respect for the past and a take-charge attitude for the future." Joy chuckled. "And now that I own my own piece of Charleston real estate and I live in the historic district, I'd like to put my love for history and tradition to work. I've got time, and I'm knowledgeable and teachable. I've looked at the historical society, but I think the preservation society suits me and I'd suit them. Why, just the other day I was on Ashley River Road," she went on, "and I stumbled on a most glorious piece of history. I was really surprised that it seemed to be empty and unloved."

"Wellington Manor." Lorilyn sighed. "A forgotten yet not neglected part of the local history, and a family that wove their very beings into the fabric of Charleston."

Joy's smile even drew Anne in. "You are a kindred spirit," she said to Lorilyn. "I saw that place and instantly thought what I would do with it, beginning with a sandblasting to bring that brick back to life. Then I'd go over it with a soft cream or ivory because the current brick blends into the backdrop far too well. I would want the place to stand out and shout 'Notice Me!' in big letters, because it's just absolutely stunning."

Horror and surprise had wiped the smile from Lorilyn's face. "You don't appreciate the original brick? A landmark to Charleston's history?"

Quiet Joy brushed that off with a skeptical expression. "Why keep things the same?" she asked in a most practical voice. "I've seen what home decorators in Texas can do with painted brick, and it absolutely brings things to life. There's this marvelous couple in Waco, and they've—"

"Don't." Lorilyn stood. "I know who you mean, and they're lovely people, but this isn't Waco, this is Charleston, and we respect our history here—the good parts, anyway—and part of that heritage is—"

"Old brick?" Joy set her glass on the table. "If we could find Byron Wellington, I might consider making an offer."

"To buy Wellington Manor?"

Joy nodded. "I have too much free time on my hands, so I'd be interested in knowing more. Of course, it's likely a dusty mess inside, but I've a mind to talk to the current owners and see what they'd want for it."

Lorilyn's expression couldn't have been more telling. "The Wellington property isn't for sale." She swallowed hard. Real hard.

"Oh, darling, everything has a price." Joy lifted her brows to underscore her words, and Anne had to choke back surprise. She had no idea that Joy could play a part so well, because she never flaunted her financial status, at least not that Anne had ever heard. "I was surprised but pleased that it didn't have landmark designation. You know how that locks things up, and for a property like this, it should surely be lived in, don't you agree? Not standing empty like a lonely sentinel peering out of the woods."

"But it isn't for sale. I mean, it can't be sold." Lorilyn looked confused as she tried to give an explanation. Her hands fluttered. "There is no owner of record at the moment."

"That's impossible," declared Joy, and then she sighed. "Unless it's involved in some sort of family dispute. Is that it? Land sakes, I've seen more property go to rack and ruin these days because folks break up or don't get along and make a mess of things."

"A family dispute, yes." Lorilyn remained standing as if weighing fight versus flight. She obviously didn't like the direction of the conversation but seemed determined to stand her ground. Literally.

Since Lorilyn wasn't going to mention the reality involved, Anne did it for her. "But Lorilyn, it's not really disputed if the heir hasn't come forward, is it? And it will revert to the preservation society next month, correct?"

Lorilyn's eyes went dark. "If someone doesn't have the presence of mind to accept an inheritance like this and leaves it standing there, year after year, letting the elements take their toll, that's not our fault, Anne. The preservation society may have been somewhat stuffy in the past—"

Anne winced because "somewhat stuffy" was a mild depiction.

"But we're different now. And understanding the love that went into an institution like Shifting Winds Home for Erring Women is a part of our history that changed things for the better. That's the history of the building that should be respected and restored."

Anne pretended confusion. "Shifting Winds?"

"The home for unwed mothers." Joy had been swirling her straw in her drink. She paused and lifted her gaze to Lorilyn. "To have thirty years of women and babies and not one fatality isn't just amazing. It's like a miracle. Any modern-day facility would be thrilled to boast those numbers, and Helen Davis did it in a time when graveyards were littered with stones naming women lost in childbirth. I can't imagine it, but I've done some research, and it seems she was a most amazing midwife."

"And that's why it should be preserved," Lorilyn insisted, but Joy's appreciation for the home's history seemed to calm her. "That's a legacy, and the story of how the parish worked to make sure most mothers were able to keep their babies and have gainful employment is a marvelous testimony to true Christian principles. Although I'm sure there were some tongues that wagged in disapproval."

Joy stood. "Aren't there always? Well, I'm a bit disappointed that we don't even have a rightful owner of record for the property. I'll keep what you've said in mind if and when I find the owner, because

I want to know more. I'm on a quest to discover all I can about Wellington Manor. I find the home and the history fascinating, and how a man of Reverend Wellington's renown was able to step away from his family legacy, take up the pastorate, and provide food, medical care, and shelter for so many cast-out women was truly a mark of greatness. Few men would have thought of such a thing, much less shouldered the burden in the face of nineteenth-century castigation. He must have been a great man."

"He seems to have had many good qualities."

Lorilyn's faint praise tweaked Anne's interest. "Do I detect a note of doubt?"

Lorilyn shook her head, but Anne knew what she'd heard. While leaping to the defense of the house, Lorilyn didn't jump on the Reverend Wellington bandwagon with any show of enthusiasm, while the entire city celebrated his progressive and loving ways as an example for all to follow.

Why?

"I saw that the gate has recently been replaced," noted Joy as they moved toward the door. "When I checked out the property online, I saw that the original was destroyed by a drunk driver several years back."

"Fortunately no one was seriously hurt, and yes, the gate has been replaced," Lorilyn acknowledged. "An act of prudence, no doubt, to keep folks from driving in. Private property should be respected."

"Well, someone must know something if they can get something like that done," Joy observed. She puffed a lock of hair out of her face as they reached the sidewalk. Beyond the roadway, heat-loving souls strolled the walkway alongside the water. A light breeze lifted the worst of the mugginess, but it was too light to make a difference unless you stayed right along the shore. "Clearly someone is seeing to things, which means either the owner is lurking quietly in the background or there's a trust set up."

"Joy, you're so wise." Anne sent her an encouraging smile. "Folks do set up trusts for all kinds of things these days."

"It's rare that I'm this taken with a historic home," Joy said to Lorilyn, and Anne was pretty sure she intensified her Texas drawl for effect. "But there's something special about a place so steeped in women-friendly history. It's like that British show with all those young nurses and those sweet babies and mothers caught in some rough situations. History, come to life."

Lorilyn stared at her. She opened her mouth as if to say something, then didn't. She swallowed hard and took a broad step back. "Best wishes on your quest, Joy."

Her formal tone indicated Joy wasn't likely to find an invitation to join the preservation society any time soon.

They were on the way back to the hospital when Anne's phone buzzed. Shirley's name showed up in the display, and Anne answered. "Hey, Shirley."

"Am I on speaker?"

"No." Anne glanced around, making sure they were quite alone while Joy lifted her brows in interest. "Do you want to be?"

"Is Joy with you?"

"Right here."

"Then yes, ma'am. But soft, okay?"

Anne adjusted the volume, and Joy drew closer. "All clear," Anne told Shirley.

"That slip of paper I dried out?"

"The landscaping thing?"

"Not landscaping," Shirley announced. "Hardscaping. D'Allesio's Hardscaping."

Anne frowned. "I don't know what that is."

"Specializing in decorative concrete, patios, walkways, and wrought iron gates."

The replaced gate.

She exchanged a quick look with Joy. "They did the gate? Who paid for it?"

"That's the clincher," whispered Shirley. "Lorilyn Cochran paid for the gate."

Lorilyn?

Anne didn't know her well, but she knew enough to know that the Cochrans were comfortable but not to the point of throwing around money to replace ornate wrought iron gates. Which might be why the replacement was a more simple model. "Odd how she failed to mention that little detail in the thirty-five minutes we just spent together." Anne looked at Joy. "Why would she do that?"

"And why does she act funny about Reverend Wellington when everyone who knew him spoke accolades about him?"

"And why does she help take care of the manor?"

"Oh, darlin', I can tell you from experience with rich folks in Atlanta," replied Shirley. "Some of them come to value their homes way more than humans. Maybe the place has become an icon to her."

"It's a house," Anne replied. "With some great history, but isn't a house just a house in the end?"

"I caught a lot of flak for selling the Atkins homestead in Houston," Joy said. "No one in the family wanted to cough up the asking price, but they didn't want me to sell it off and move either. I didn't listen to them, but it wasn't comfortable. I'm probably off the guest list for some Atkins family get-togethers, but at some point you just have to do what needs to be done. Whatever the cost. And a good shake-up now and again can be a good thing. Clears the cobwebs, like Regina likes to say."

"But why would she replace that gate?" wondered Anne, and Joy met her gaze straight on.

"Let's go ask."

Chapter Ten

THEY WALKED STRAIGHT OVER TO the preservation society offices, a less than ten-minute walk from where they'd talked with Shirley.

Lorilyn wasn't there. Or she was refusing to open the door.

Either way, there was no asking her in person, and Anne didn't want to use the phone. People could hide reactions on the phone. Not so much in person.

"Foiled." Joy made a face. "I don't like being foiled."

"I'm beginning to understand that better, and it only makes me like you more." Anne laughed and tucked her arm through Joy's. "How about we go grab some fish and chips over on Ashley River Road and then pop in on Shirley and Regina? I feel rushed," she confessed as they headed toward Anne's parking space. "Not just because Addie will be coming home on Sunday, but because this will is a legal document. If we don't find the truth about Byron, then it all comes down to the preservation society. I hate to think that Lorilyn has something up her sleeve, but I'm pretty sure that's exactly what's going on."

Joy climbed into the front seat and snapped her seat belt into place as her phone chimed a very musical text alert. "Evelyn's free. She found out something worth noting. Where are we?"

"Tell her we're on our way for fish and chips. If it's all right with Shirley and Regina, we can gather at their place with food in about forty-five minutes. Use food bribe as needed."

Shirley's smiley emoji came through with no need for a bribe, but Joy told her about the food run anyway. "We don't want her or Regina thinking they need to make us something," she said as they crossed the river and took the Fielding Connector to Ashley River Road. Joy called in an order, and by the time they pulled into the restaurant's pickup parking area, they only had five minutes to wait for their fish and chips to be ready. They drove straight to Shirley's with the amazing array of scents filling the car until there was no choice but to eat a few fries.

Evelyn tucked her car very snugly behind Anne's and hopped out of the driver's seat looking quite pleased with herself right after Anne turned the engine off. "Mystery man outed!" she declared as they hurried up Shirley's steps. "Wait until you hear this."

"Food first?" asked Anne.

"News first. I'll be quick," promised Evelyn. They went inside, set the bags on Regina's old oak table, and everyone gathered around. After greetings were over, Evelyn reached into the pocket of her stylish pants and withdrew a folded paper. "Meet Cabbie Joe."

Cabbie Joe? Anne frowned as she recognized the man in the picture as the one at Wellington Manor. "Joe Brown? Abel Jackson's friend?"

"Now known as 'Cabbie Joe,' the morning DJ for C-Town Radio, soft rock of the seventies—"

"Eighties and nineties," said Anne with her. "What's a popular DJ doing in Byron Wellington's house?"

"No clue." Evelyn breathed deeply, then sighed. "But it's him. He looks older in person, so this shot must be a few years old. Sick, maybe? Lost his apartment? Mental illness?"

"I can't deny those thoughts ran through my mind when we met up with him," said Anne. "Does he live there for real? Or was he just staying there after a rough night? We all know that Charleston has its share of rough nights."

"We need to go see him," said Shirley. "And I'm obligated to test these French fries because quality control is important." She snatched two fries from the container and sighed happily then handed a couple to Regina.

"What time does he get out of work?" Anne snitched another fry too.

"The show airs from six until ten, so if we stake out the studio from ten o'clock on, we should be able to corner him."

"I'm off this Thursday because the hospital needs me to sub in on Friday," said Anne. "Hair trim at eight thirty, so I can stalk this guy with good hair."

"Good hair is empowering," said Regina. "But you can't go alone. Can any of you other gals go with her?"

"I can," said Joy. "Shirley and Evelyn are both working Thursday morning."

"And I'm off on Friday," said Shirley. "But the three of you are working."

"Then it's me and Anne Thursday morning," said Joy.

Regina fanned herself, then crossed to the cupboard. "I'm getting plates because this smells like a feast. I like catfish well enough, but I love these English-style fish dinners. And here's vinegar for the chips, done in proper style."

It was a feast, and they'd discussed a lot tonight. When Anne shared Lorilyn's reaction to Joy's ideas, Evelyn turned toward Joy, concerned. "Lorilyn's husband plays in a Thursday night card club with James, and he's a delightful fellow. Lorilyn might be a little caught up in history—"

Joy snorted at the word *little*.

Evelyn acknowledged that with a nod. "Okay, quite absorbed with history, but she's a nice person. Really nice. This is out-of-character behavior for her I think, and I can't help but wonder why."

"We wondered the same thing," said Anne. "Does she help other historic properties? Or just this one?"

"I know the gals who do the filing and typing at the preservation society office," said Regina. "And our gal Marnie—she goes to Mother Emmanuel most times, 'cept when she's over at City of Grace with her sister—she sets up government things to help them out."

"Grant applications?" asked Anne, and Regina nodded.

"Yes, those, and she has to do them up quick before money runs out, but she's gotten them a lot of notice the past five years. I expect Marnie would tell us this and that as long as it matters. She's not one to gossip."

"I'd love to meet her," Anne told her. "But I can't very well go over there when Lorilyn is around. Way too awkward."

"I'll see if Marnie can meet us," said Shirley. "We don't dare meet in the Grove—"

"This week's heat and humidity make that a nonoption anyway," said Joy. "I'm willing to sweat for a cause but only to a certain degree, and they're predicting ninety-ninety. Way out of my comfort zone, y'all."

"What about meeting at Ginger's?" Anne suggested. "It's close by, and it was fairly quiet when we met there today."

"I'll see when she's available," Shirley promised. She sighed as she looked at the empty plate before her. "Thanks so much for a great treat, y'all. For some reason fish and chips makes me think of the little boy with the loaves and fishes in the Bible. And that always reminds me to be grateful for good food and good friends. I never expected to find such good, quick friends when I moved here, and you've made it a blessing. For both of us," she added with a smile at Regina. "Of course I wasn't surprised that Mama had made such good friends over her years of working at Mercy."

Her words inspired Regina's smile. "I have been blessed, for certain. I loved most of my time at Mercy, but there were spots here and there that weren't good. Why is it we remember those spots so well and forget the weeks and months of goodness? The memory's a funny thing. Y'all have been talking and reminding me of that young doctor and that terrible accident, but it's the way Max Schlater threatened him that I've been thinking of lately."

Anne leaned forward, surprised, because Regina hadn't mentioned this before. "Dr. Schlater threatened Dr. Wellington?"

"Not like it was a big surprise, knowing Max's history," Regina continued. "He was born a bully and stayed that way all his life. I stayed out of his way because he had no love lost for people of color, but he also had no love lost for anyone who threatened his position. And that Wellington fellow must have unnerved him a fair piece, because Max gave him a tongue-lashing like you wouldn't believe about a month after those boys went home to Jesus. I didn't like Max before, and I liked him even less since. Fortunately I worked downstairs and he worked on Trauma and our paths didn't have to cross all that often."

"What did he say to Dr. Wellington, Mama?" Shirley looked just as surprised as Anne felt.

"I remember it like it was yesterday. He told him that a man like him, that relied more on his ego than science, should spare the world his ineptitude and leave medicine altogether. He called him a loser, and then he shouted, 'If I could, I'd have you out of here now. Today. And I would make sure you never practiced medicine again, because you will be the ruination of this trauma team and this hospital, and I've let every director know how I feel. And when it comes down to you or me?' Then he kind of leaned in. I couldn't see Dr. Wellington's face, but I saw Max's, and never have I seen an uglier expression on anyone's face." Regina drew a breath, her brow drawn, and her eyes dark with trouble. "'You are worthless, Wellington, for all your big name and lofty credentials. You've always skated through because you've happened to be in the right place at the right time and no one died. It seems your winning run is over.'"

Chills ran up and down Anne's arms. She crossed them to warm herself, despite the mild temps inside the house. "How cruel."

"Well. That's Max."

Anne knew the older doctor was disliked by many, but to have been allowed to carry on like this for so long? What did that say about the administrators? About her beloved hospital?

"They made him retire, you know." Evelyn had her arms crossed too.

Anne shook her head. "I didn't know that."

"Ten years back, as the new administrators were coming on board, they told him he needed to leave or be let go. Oh, it was hush-hush, and the floor held a retirement thing for him and no one attended. That was a kerfuffle of the highest sort, so that's why he has an office in the professional building as a consulting doctor. When the new admins came on board, they wanted a clean slate, and Garrison came to us with a similar frame of mind. There's a man who's worth some admiration."

"He's wonderful," Anne agreed.

She drove Joy home half an hour later. The streets were just beginning to darken. Streetlights flickered on, the long days of summer giving them reprieve, and as she pulled up in front of Joy's house, she yawned.

Then she stopped yawning.

Her mouth dropped open for another reason. Joy's front yard was bordered by a beautiful foot-high redbrick wall. And the pretty brick was now marred with paint—

Cream-toned paint—

And two simple words were painted in the same color high on her beautiful front door, stark against the black finish. LIKE IT?

Anne's heart nearly stopped.

Joy's eyes had grown round and she just sat and stared for what seemed like long, drawn-out seconds, then she yanked out her phone, hit 911, and spoke crisply to the call center operator. "My home has been vandalized," she said. "And I'm reasonably sure I know exactly who did it. Lorilyn Cochran, the head of the preservation society."

Chapter Eleven

"JOY. YOUR HOUSE." ANNE COULDN'T believe what she was seeing.

She touched nothing. She'd watched enough BritBox TV to know that she didn't want to contaminate a crime scene, but was Joy right? Had they bothered Lorilyn so much that she charged right over here while they enjoyed crispy hot fish and chips?

Anne doubted it. Lorilyn wasn't that kind of person. She was passionate about her love for history and preserving parts of it, but she wasn't reactionary. Of course, if there was something else going on, like she and Joy suspected, maybe their visit would spawn a reaction like this?

"I can't believe she did this." If Joy were a cartoon character, steam would be puffing from her ears. She stormed around and around her front lawn, and when the police car rolled to a stop, she charged right out to meet them.

Anne would have described Joy as quiet. Mild-mannered. Even-tempered.

But her friend was none of the above right now, and if it wasn't such an in-your-face and hard-to-clean crime, she'd have teased her about it.

Jimbo Carson met Joy at the open gate. "Miss Atkins, is this your place?" he asked, and she grabbed him in a hug. Jimbo was one of the local cops who regularly stopped in at the gift store for Joy's free coffee and conversation.

"Jimbo, look what they've done," she exclaimed. "I'm fit to be tied. I can't believe someone would go to these extremes to warn us off a case."

"A case?" He lifted his brows as Anne moved forward. He likely recognized her right off because Jimbo often accompanied ambulances into the Mercy ER. "And Miss Anne, you too? What's going on, ladies?"

Joy gave him a brief explanation, and Anne breathed a sigh of relief when she left out details of their investigation, because she was pretty sure the experienced officer would think they were either silly or in danger, and Anne wouldn't appreciate either assignation. "It had to be Lorilyn," finished Joy. "There's no one else in this world who knew we were talking about painting bricks, and she was appalled at the notion. I declare I've almost got the urge to buy the Wellington house and paint it cream out of spite. Although I think I'd go more ivory, now that I see this," she finished.

Jimbo had let her talk. He was a patient man, the kind that handled worried families with a much-needed calm, and when she finished spewing, he offered some good advice. "Let me check into things. I'm no detective, but over the years I've found that the most obvious answer is often the least likely, because folks'll set up other folks to drive suspicion away from themselves. It's not an unusual circumstance."

"Except there was no one else around to hear it," Joy reminded him.

"You were in a secluded room?"

She frowned. "Well, no. We were over at the East Bay Café. Ginger's place."

"And no one else came in while you were talking?"

"A few to-go orders. And there were two more tables, a bit away."

"And who was at those tables?"

Joy's frown deepened. So did Anne's. She'd been so focused on Joy's exchange with Lorilyn, that she never thought to check who was near them. "I have no idea."

"And that's why we don't dare assume," he told her kindly. "I know Miss Cochran, and she's a nice lady. And she's about five-four, wouldn't you say?"

"Anne's height, yes."

"Well, I look at this writing on the door, and if Anne were writing with spray paint, it would be here, wouldn't it?" Jimbo indicated Anne's shoulder level. "This is nearly a foot above that, and that means the person was likely taller. At least five foot ten, I'd say, maybe even six feet. I mean, Miss Cochran could have brought something to stand on to try to throw us off, but I doubt someone would take the time to do that in broad daylight."

Joy sighed, resigned. "You're right. Then who?"

Jimbo folded his arms and frowned. "I don't know, but someone wants you to back off, Miss Joy."

"Just Joy," she told him firmly. "We've had this discussion at the gift shop."

"We have," he acknowledged with a grin, "but my mama taught me respect, and it's a hard thing to unlearn." He sobered. "I'd like to check inside and around back to make sure nothing else is going on," he told them.

Joy handed him the key.

"Now you ladies wait right here," he said.

After trying the front door, he unlocked it and stepped onto the piazza. There were two entries to the house from the piazza. Anne watched him check the one that led into the living area then use the key and open the door to the kitchen.

Motion lights blinked on, flooding the entry and kitchen with light. When Jimbo disappeared into the house Anne and Joy made their way into the kitchen. Nothing looked out of place, and they could hear Jimbo's footsteps on the floor above. When he came back downstairs, he frowned when he saw them waiting. "I do believe I asked you to stay outside," he scolded. "What if there'd been someone lurking inside?"

"Well, the doors were all locked, making that unlikely, and I wanted to see how you do this," Joy said. "It wasn't nearly as dramatic as on TV. They go to extremes, don't you think?"

"Well, if I thought there was an armed person inside, I would have called backup and proceeded with more caution," he told her. "But the locked doors and no sign of forced entry gave me some sense of security. I'm going to warn both of you," he added in a firmer tone of voice. "Whoever did this apparently just wanted to alarm you. But sometimes people go to the next level if their warnings don't work, and I don't want anything happening to either of you. Whatever you're doing, be careful. Okay?"

Joy nodded. "We will, Jimbo. And thank you for coming right over."

"Miss Anne?" He turned her way.

Anne agreed too. "We'll be careful. Is Joy okay to stay here?"

"Well, that depends on how she feels about it. She's got a good set of locks and a security system."

"I'm not letting someone scare me out of my new home," declared Joy. "A little bit of paint doesn't worry me, but I'll be careful. I'm going to think about who might have been in that coffee shop. I sure wish we'd paid attention."

"Call if there's any further trouble," Jimbo told them.

"We will." After he pulled away from the curb, Joy turned to Anne. "I can't believe we didn't look around us. I never considered such a thing, Anne, but he's right. Lorilyn wouldn't have been able to spray paint up there."

Anne agreed, but she took a different tack. "No, but the fact that whoever did this didn't think of that is the best clue we've gotten. We know this person is tall, and that's significant. And maybe not practiced at setting up other people, because he or she didn't think of that. They just painted at their own height."

"Tall or not, Lorilyn Cochran is hiding something," Joy replied. "We both know that. But since she's not the only one, we'll figure out both. Is that Cabbie Joe guy tall?"

Anne nodded.

"That puts him on the list."

"Except would he be getting coffee on East Bay Street? At the very same time we happened to be there?"

The unlikelihood of that wrinkled Joy's brow. "Probably not, and I'm too tired to think straight, so I'm going to go all Scarlett O'Hara on this and worry about it in the morning. I want to be awake when we go on that ghost hunt. Good night, my friend."

Anne climbed into the car and waited until Joy texted her that she was tucked inside and the doors were locked, then she drove north toward home, but she wasn't yawning now.

Who had targeted Joy?

And why didn't they want her checking into Wellington Manor?

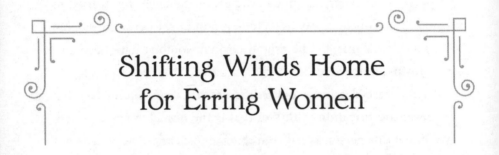

Shifting Winds Home for Erring Women

October 1894

The air felt wrong.

Helen had heard reports of a bad storm in Georgia. Travelers had claimed to have outrun a tempest that could rival last year's treacherous storm. That storm had claimed nearly two thousand lives of poor folk living on the islands, eking a living as best they could. If it weren't for the likes of Clara Barton and her workers, the remaining residents might be stranded and homeless still. But one woman's intervention had turned the tide of hopelessness into a flurry of action, and the islands were populated again. Only less so.

But another storm, the third this year? So soon after the last one? And why were repeated storms coming their way?

She didn't have answers. She evacuated their new school and brought everyone back to the main house, including the groundskeeper and his family. They were well stocked with provisions. She and Colleen had taught the residents how to can all varieties of fruits and vegetables from the lush early gardens. The larder was full, but last year's storm had left a hole in so many hearts. The phosphate mines, guaranteed to bring big money to a growing metropolis, had flooded in the storm's path. Many had failed to reopen. And this year, past storms had already driven water levels to unusual heights for October.

Miri sought her out once the secondary students were accounted for. "Do you think it will be bad, Mama?"

"A question with no answer as yet," Helen said. "But I pray that one day we shall have machines that can see storms as they come. Maybe even why they come where they come and give folks time to get ready."

"Like all those people last year," whispered Miriam. She leaned her head against Helen's, and she didn't have to stretch or bend to do it. They were of the same height now, although Miriam's coloring was different. Darker hair and brows, and an arch to those brows that offered expression to her features. Other than that, she resembled her mother. "I couldn't imagine that, Mama. So many souls gone. Just like that."

"A tragedy, darling. Absolutely." She laid an arm around Miriam's shoulders. "We pray for safety for all and we help those in need, for such is the calling of God's people."

"Miriam?" The newly hired teacher came their way. "Can you help us settle the books we brought into the library? The reverend's children are helping, and Jacob could benefit from your gentle guidance."

Jacob, who had been a tender little fellow, was still gentle of heart but also all boy, and big, busy movements had become the order of the day since he turned eight.

"Happily, for the library is one of my favorite rooms," Miriam exclaimed. She hugged her mother and went off.

When the storm barreled through midday, the wild combination of lashing wind, rain, thunder, and lightning cast a dark pall over the beautiful home.

Robert fought the storm to check on them in the first hour. "How are you faring?" he asked when Helen and Colleen opened the wide kitchen door to let him in. One person wasn't a match for the wind and the heavy door. Neither woman could have held it alone.

"Well," she told him once they'd shut the door.

"And the children?"

"All well," she assured him, and when his gaze sought hers for even more reassurance, she smiled. "Why don't you stay here until the storm passes? Is the rectory truly safe?"

"Not as solid as this, but it's compact enough to be all right," he told her. "Still, when storms erupt, I like knowing the children are all here, where two generations of previous Wellingtons stayed safe and sound."

"A smart selection, sir." Colleen poured him a mug of coffee. "I just made this, and I expect you could use a cup."

"I could, indeed, and then I'll head back up the way. We kept the church open for travelers and locals who fear the storm's wrath."

"Calming fears is something you and God have in common," Helen said. He left after his coffee, and she could only see him a few feet up the walk before his form was shrouded by wind-driven rain.

"He is a good man." Colleen was putting hard-boiled eggs in a bowl to go with a simple supper. "We are blessed to have him. Both in the church and here."

"Amen."

"And every now and again I wonder if he will marry again," Colleen went on. She'd finished her eggs and was chopping celery for salad.

Helen kept her eyes downcast. "I think we shall leave the business of that to the man in question."

"Of course." Colleen agreed in word, but as she kept assembling the chicken and celery and chopped nuts, she said, "He's not a man of significant age, he's quite handsome, he's a wonderful rector, and—"

She stopped suddenly, and when Helen looked her way, Colleen's expression—

One of knowing—

Caught her unawares.

Her heart sped up.

She was no Jane Eyre, leaning on and waiting for the kind words of her employer, but two spots of warmth in her cheeks betrayed her. "I will fetch the bread."

"Of course." Colleen said no more, but as they worked side by side, Helen felt her gaze twice. Each time she schooled herself to keep her eyes down, on her work.

Talk would be her undoing, therefore there could be no talk. No thoughts of what-ifs or wherefores. When the sandwiches were made she left the kitchen with nothing more than the whisper of her skirts shifting against the shelves.

Chapter Twelve

"SHE'S TALL." JOY WHISPERED THE words as she and Anne hurried over to the Ghost Walk starting point the next evening.

"About five foot ten with those shoes," noted Anne. "Can she really walk the whole tour in those?"

"Stabilizer arches," Joy replied. "They make all the difference. Like walking in those heeled boots. The right arch is clutch."

Anne knew little about arches, but she really liked Tula's shoes. Right now, however, she was watching for Tula's reaction when she spotted them.

Tula turned around—

Anne's heart sped up.

No reaction. None. Nothing. Nada. Zilch.

Anne couldn't believe it, and she didn't understand it right up until a man to their left began calling out the names of ticketed participants.

They had a list.

That's why Tula didn't react. She knew they were coming and was prepared, and for a woman who did community theater, she hid her reaction well.

"Ladies and gentlemen, I want to welcome you to tonight's Ghost Tour. This isn't a walk to convince you that ghosts are real or that we subscribe to that idea. Instead it's to open your mind to our rich history and reveal to you..."

She made eye contact with Anne for a brief moment.

"Not the mysteries surrounding our city but the truths that lay hidden in the ashes of massive pyres."

Anne looked around. The small crowd watched, eyes wide.

"In the hidden corners of narrowed streets and thin alleys."

It seemed that no one breathed.

"And of course the most sacred corners of all, where we trod gently through the graves of our beloved dead." Her tone and her expression sent a chill through Anne, and in today's muggy air, the chill felt good.

"We'll walk."

People nodded.

"We'll talk."

That made sense to the group, it seemed, but then Tula leaned forward. So far forward as if needing to be close to the circle of people. She dropped her voice low. Really low. "And sometimes we'll talk softly. Very softly. The need to be loud can interfere with your thoughts. What you see. And what you perceive." She swept the group a look, then breathed softly. Purposely. And then she aimed her gaze right at Anne again. And she said, "Madam, will you walk?"

The reference to the old Mary Stewart suspense novel wasn't lost on Anne. She loved mystery and suspense, she always had, and she'd read that book multiple times. She'd often thought of becoming a mystery writer. Time and life had held different paths for her, but something about the challenge of Tula's words made Anne lift her chin and gaze right into the taller woman's eyes. "Absolutely. And maybe at some point, we'll have a talk as well."

Tula's eyes flashed, but she recovered herself quickly and laughed. "If you have a love for mystery, we'd have much to talk about, I'm sure." She moved ahead, and she didn't just use her voice to describe what people were seeing. She used her arms. Her legs. A fluid walk, a graceful personage, quite different from her everyday appearance at the hospital.

Anne and Joy slipped back behind a couple of people as the sidewalk narrowed. "She's good," whispered Joy. "She's got just the right amount of pizzazz."

"She was great as Miss Hannigan in *Annie*," Anne whispered back. "But she outdid herself in the Hitchcock series they did several years back. When it comes to mystery and heroines, she's done several of their leads. Not so much now." She stopped for a moment when the person in front of them turned around and frowned at them. "She's older. And we don't get down here so often now with Addie. But Tula's not afraid to get into a part, and you need that for suspense and intrigue."

They stayed quiet then, as Tula kept the group's attention through voice, movement, and story.

Seeing her in this light, it wasn't difficult to imagine a young doctor and a cafeteria worker having a relationship. But what happened when Byron ended that relationship?

That's what Anne wanted to know.

She hoped to grab an impromptu conversation with Tula when the engaging tour was over, but as people began disbanding, walking in this direction and that, a car pulled up to the corner and before Anne and Joy could get closer, Tula opened the passenger door and slipped inside. Just as quickly, the driver eased into the diminished traffic, rounded a corner, and was heading north, but not before Anne noticed something strange.

The man driving the car looked a whole lot like Byron Wellington looked thirty years ago.

Shirley and Evelyn met Anne and Joy early Wednesday morning at Ginger's. The place was always hopping by seven a.m., and Joy had the sense to send in their order through her phone app so they wouldn't waste time. Shirley went in, grabbed their drink tray, and slipped back out as the line grew. "I owe you, Joy Atkins!" she exclaimed as she took a deep breath of coffee-scented air. "Mama was in good form this morning, and she was longing to share about every old story known to mankind. But I had missed Snooze and hit Dismiss, and that put me a quarter-hour behind when I woke back up. Thank you, Joy." She smiled as she puffed a cooling breath over the cup's narrow opening. "This will hit the spot."

"So what did you find out last night?" Evelyn wasted no time talking about coffee. "I took my sisters on the Bulldog Ghost Tour years ago, and it was full of fascinating history. And some theatrics," she added, smiling.

"Well, Tula does them proud," said Joy. "She's amazing. And Anne told me she's great in community theater, but that wasn't the showstopper."

"No?"

"She got picked up by a young man who looked a lot like Byron Wellington," said Anne. She kept her voice soft, just in case. She didn't want a repeat of what happened two days before. "Enough like him to be his son. So maybe there was more to their relationship than anyone knew."

Evelyn lifted her brows. "Well, that's been known to happen, but would Tula be able to keep a secret like that all this time? Surely someone else would notice the resemblance and it would become hospital gossip. Wouldn't it?" She made a rueful face. "Everything else does, it seems."

"She's taken time off in the past," said Anne.

"But then she came back." Evelyn didn't appear to be buying it. "She could have worked at another hospital facility. She didn't have to come back here. And Regina said she wanted to try her hand at full-time acting, so I assumed that's what she was doing. Where does she live?"

"She's listed in an apartment complex out on Route 17, past the Citadel Mall, and she takes the bus in. That's nearly an hour ride, but it gives her enough distance that if she were raising a child, no one here might know."

"A mother not talking about her child?" Shirley sounded doubtful.

"Well, if the child is the son of the missing trauma surgeon, one might want to keep it under wraps." Joy sipped her coffee, and the taste must have been wonderful, because it made her smile. "It wasn't just that he picked her up. It's how she just slipped to the curb and disappeared into the car."

"She got away from you." Evelyn laughed.

"She sure did," admitted Anne with a rueful sigh. "Despite my years of fascination with mysteries and suspense, I wasn't bold enough to get in the way. Or even think to be in the way to block her escape. My bad."

"She's pretty easily cornered at the hospital, right?" Evelyn steadied her coffee as they started down the walk.

"At work?" Anne interrupted her sip of coffee. "I can't approach her at work."

"Because?" Shirley asked, genuinely puzzled.

"It would be wrong. It's on company time. It's—"

"Easy?" Evelyn laughed again, and Shirley joined in. "You're not interrogating her. You're asking a legitimate question. Unless you think she killed him, in which case you might be putting yourself in danger."

"Grave danger," added Joy, helpfully. "Pun intended. I'd offer an opinion if I knew her, but Shirley and I are the new kids on the block."

"I'll ask her." Evelyn put an end to the back and forth. "She won't expect it of me. She walks through the records hallway at least once every day as she distributes the baked goods to the coffee shop and kiosks, and I'll see what she says. If she knows something, I'll get an inkling. She may be a good actress, but if she's that tied to Byron by either death, a child, or both—"

Anne cringed despite her best intentions of being cool as a cucumber.

Evelyn winked. "I don't think she killed anyone, but in any case, Byron's days for the bequest are numbered, and we might be the only people who care. So it's up to us, and I haven't done my fair share on this, so I'll talk to Tula today. That will give us some input before you and Joy waylay Cabbie Joe tomorrow. And FYI"—she addressed Joy and Anne specifically—"it would be a shame to lock Joe away for murder, because he's a huge Billy Joel fan. He knows all the words to 'Scenes From an Italian Restaurant,' and people who love that song aren't the kind who murder. In my opinion."

Anne burst out laughing. "I'm not laughing because you're funny," she said finally, when she could catch her breath. "I'm laughing because you're right. Anyone can sing 'Uptown Girl,' but 'Scenes From an Italian Restaurant' is a true test of fandom. How about if we meet you gals at Shirley's tomorrow afternoon? We'll fill you in on Cabbie Joe, and you tell us about Tula and—"

Anne stopped. Pointed ahead.

The thick trees from a nearby home kept them in shadow as they approached the walkway leading toward the Angel of Mercy and her pretty rose-and-ivory-toned garden. Just beyond the angel, hidden from the hospital windows, Dr. Schlater was raising his voice to someone. Anne couldn't make out his words, but his intent to bully and badger was clear. A moment later he strode toward the professional building. He moved so fast and strong that his bag slapped his leg in angry fashion. At that moment Anne saw the person he'd been berating.

Tula Manchester.

And it was clear from the tears on her cheeks that whatever the mean-spirited doctor said, he'd hit his mark.

Evelyn wasted no time.

Without a word, she hurried down the walk.

Anne exchanged looks with the other women. "I'm going to pray that Evelyn's gentle warmth and compassion are just what Tula needs right now. Whatever that man said to her was hurtful. One way or another, he needs to be taken down a peg. Now we just need to figure out how to do it."

Shirley and Joy stared after the belligerent man, then turned back to Anne in unison. "I'm in." Shirley kept her voice calm, but there was fire smoldering in her dark brown eyes. "Browbeating is not allowed in the Shirley Bashore rule book, so taking this guy down a notch will feel good."

"And having dealt with a few stupid wranglers in my day, I'm quite on board with this," added Joy in her gentler tone. "Wilson didn't tolerate less than solid respect for women, and my mama told me 'Girl, you may be small, but you're strong. Stand your ground and you'll do just fine.'"

"I like your mother," declared Anne.

"You would have. She looked mild, but she was a force to be reckoned with. She wasn't afraid to run cattle or bake bread, and folks respected her because she never ran from a fight. Nor have I."

"I saw that the other night. Now if we can figure out who was messing around your house—"

"I'm having security cameras installed first thing tomorrow," Joy told her as the three women went through the hospital doors near the discharge area. With July temperatures and humidity still soaring, the indoor halls offered a much cooler walk to the lobby and the emergency room area beyond. Joy headed straight to the gift shop to get it ready for opening, Anne moved to the large, circular front desk and information center, and Shirley hurried toward the ER. She was nearly to the big dividing doors when a voice rang out, loud enough for Anne to hear. "Nurse Bashore."

Anne had tucked her purse into a locked drawer in a file cabinet, designed for this purpose.

Her gaze shot up.

Chad Barnhardt was striding toward Shirley, and he looked disgruntled. "Running late?"

"Not late at all, Doctor." Shirley kept her tone easy. "I've got six minutes on my watch, plenty of time to get into place for the shift change advisory. Is your watch off?"

She didn't raise her voice.

She didn't call him out.

But her calm seemed to annoy him. He raised his left arm. "My watch is never off. My watch is—"

He stared down, then lifted his gaze to the lobby clock, donated by a local business. He stared at the 7:24 while it switched to 7:25.

Chagrin darkened his face, but Shirley didn't gloat. Watching the exchange, Anne was pretty sure she wouldn't have been able to keep her cool like Shirley did.

Shirley waved a hand like all was okay and approached the automatic door. "We'll make this five minutes count, Doctor. And mercy, doesn't the coolness of that AC feel good? It's a steam bath outside."

Dr. Barnhardt had no choice.

He glanced around as if checking to see who had noticed his gaffe, and Anne saw that everyone suddenly got busy.

Then, chin down, he followed Shirley through the doors.

"That man can be such a bear," whispered Aurora Kingston to Anne as she double-checked her volunteer ledger. "I wouldn't be able to work with him, that's for certain. I don't know how Shirley does it."

Anne thought back to Shirley's comments earlier that week. She signed in and drew on a pink smock with her volunteer pin attached. "Prayer," she told Aurora.

Aurora rolled her eyes.

Anne wasn't about to stand down. "She prays for him. For all of her coworkers and patients. And you see the results."

"It will take more than something that simple to make a good person out of Chad," Aurora retorted. "It's disheartening to think that people who come to our ER have to deal with that."

Anne couldn't let that pass. She stood tall and faced the volunteer coordinator. "Our ER is amazing. Chad might be a little gruff sometimes, but he is one of the best ER doctors in the area. He's trained some amazing doctors and nurses who've had the honor to work with him. He does come on too strong sometimes, but people don't rush to the ER for hand-holding. They come for medical help of the highest order, and that's what they get. No one can say otherwise."

Aurora pursed her lips then moved away, but not without one parting shot. "There's nothing wrong with being a decent human *and* being a great doctor. He doesn't have to be Mr. Congeniality, but he could at least be polite. And you know it." She stalked off, looking way more like Chad Barnhardt than she realized, and Anne decided then and there to put Aurora on the prayer list next to Chad. If prayer and kindness could help, she was 100 percent determined to give her colleagues both.

NEED TO SEE YOU. NOON? Evelyn's text came through midmorning.

Anne texted back quickly between discharging patients. No. 12:45? COVERING LUNCHES OVER HERE.

It was several minutes before a return text came through. 12:45. An adorable female sleuth emoji followed. The sight of it made Anne laugh out loud. At twelve forty she hurried across the lobby's second floor, down the stairs, and into the vintage wing. When she got to the records desk, one of the new interns was scrolling her phone.

Anne fought the urge to scold her, and before she could even ask for Evelyn, the young woman gestured toward the Vault. "She's in the dungeon, which is now cleaner than it's probably been in fifty years, and just so you know, that wasn't in my job description."

Anne sent her a bright smile. "It rarely is. But things must get done, eh?" She hurried into the tucked-away room.

Fresher air greeted her.

And so did Tula Manchester.

Anne looked at Tula.

Then Evelyn.

Then Tula again. "So we meet again."

Tula sighed. She brushed a lock of silvering honey-toned hair from her face and stood. "I know what you're doing."

Anne didn't have to pretend confusion, because she was genuinely confused. "About what?"

"Dr. Schlater and me."

It took everything to hide a reaction to Tula's words, but she did it. "Well—"

"He's an angry and vindictive man. Please, just drop it. All of it. He's already out of the hospital, and I love my job. I need my job. If word of this gets out, I could be fired."

"I don't want that to happen," said Anne, wishing Evelyn could give her a clue what Tula was talking about. But Evelyn simply went along with it. Like Anne was doing. "But why was he yelling at you this morning?"

"Because he heard that you were asking questions about me and about Byron. He said if I talk to anyone, he'll personally see to it that my job is gone. His wife's cousin owns the Spirits of Magnolia Tour, and that six months of money is crucial to my income, especially now that the city has gotten so expensive. Please. Just stop."

Anne couldn't make that promise. "What does he have to fear, Tula?"

She shook her head. "He's been angry for a long time. He thinks the system is against him. He's never been able to accept any responsibility when things go wrong, but that's not the point. Even though he's not on staff, he's got power. Way more than people think, and he doesn't have much of a conscience, if any. Just leave it alone." She sighed when she stood. "I appreciate that you care, but you have to leave it alone."

"I don't know that we can," Evelyn said. "A man shouldn't get away with threatening your livelihood. What's next? Your life?"

Tula frowned. "You don't get it. Neither of you do, but it's not me that I'm worried about. I can take care of myself, but not everyone is like that, so if you'd just forget about whatever you know or think you know, that would be good. For me. And probably for you."

"Is that a threat?"

"Not from me," she said. "But Max can't be trusted. I know that from personal experience. If you're smart you'll take my advice. Nobody around here wants to find themselves on Max Schlater's bad side. Nobody."

Should I bring up Byron? Anne wondered.

She should, because did she really have a choice? "Tula, is Dr. Schlater still upset about Dr. Wellington? You and he were rather close before he left the hospital."

Tula's jaw firmed, and she frowned. "Byron Wellington was one of the nicest, smartest people I've ever known. He should have become a cornerstone for modern medicine here. He was sharp. Strong. Innovative. But his presence was a threat to—"

"Dr. Schlater."

"Not just him. There was a band of doctors who—" She paused. Sighed. Then drew a deep breath. "They wanted Byron gone. He was showing them up. Schlater didn't work alone, he rarely does, and I should have seen that earlier. And he never forgets. Byron faced tough odds here. More than any skilled practitioner should have to face."

"You loved him." Anne made the statement as an observation. Tula's expression and voice made her feelings clear.

"We loved each other. But I couldn't help him when he needed it the most." Her gaze dropped to the floor, as if defeated. "He left me, and I couldn't blame him. I wasn't what he needed."

"What did he need, Tula?"

Anne's question jerked Tula out of her melancholy. She straightened her shoulders, raised her chin, and faced Anne. "Respect. And no matter how hard he tried, he didn't get that here. And now he's gone." She pivoted and marched straight for the door, then swung it wide. "And we can never get him back."

The click of the door punctuated the words.

"Gone?" Anne turned toward Evelyn. "Does she mean gone as in gone? Or gone as in…" She swallowed hard. "Dead?"

Evelyn broke her rule against frowning. "I don't know. And I didn't dare ask her about the young man you saw."

The young man who resembled Byron Wellington.

"What power does Schlater have over her?" wondered Anne.

Evelyn's frown deepened. "Another question I can't answer. I can't imagine them having a relationship."

Anne couldn't either.

But Tula feared Schlater. That much was clear. The question was: Why?

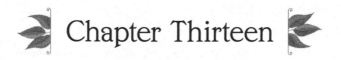

Chapter Thirteen

"Nana, I'm having the best time!" Addie's vibrant voice was just what Anne needed that evening. "This is Lady Belle," she went on and pointed the phone toward a gorgeous bay mare. "She's been my horse all week, and she really loves me, and I love her, and I think it's really good for kids to have horses, don't you? I'm sending you a video of all the fun things we've done together. You'll love it, Nana!"

Anne recognized the setup right off. "I don't think the city allows horses, honey. We don't have enough room."

"But that's the best, Nana!" Addie exclaimed. "We can keep the horse at a stable, that's what the other kids do, like some of them, not all of them," she explained with all the seven-year-old earnestness she could muster. "They said there's stable places that keep your horse for you and feed it and *everything*. But I did learn how to clean up poop. They made us," she added, but with horse-savvy nonchalance. "I didn't even mind, because horses like to be clean. It makes them happy. And Lady Belle is so happy. I think she loves me a lot," she finished, and the winsome note in her voice tipped the scales in her favor.

Lili had never explored horseback riding as a child, but Addie was her own person, so maybe she was right. Maybe there were affordable stables in the Charleston area. It wouldn't hurt to check it out. "I'm so glad you're having fun, darling. And I can't wait to see you on Sunday. We'll have your most special supper, and you can tell us all about the camp."

"I will, Nana! Love you!"

"I love you too, darling!" Anne blew kisses at the phone. Addie blew them back, and when the connection ended, satisfaction made Anne smile.

She'd been overly cautious with Liliana. She realized that now. Partially because they'd lost Ariane, and partially because she felt like the entire congregation was focused on her and her mothering skills, which meant Lili better behave.

She'd learned her lessons the hard way when her relationship with her beautiful and accomplished daughter became so strained that Lili started avoiding her. It had taken time and prayer and maturity for them to recognize the wedge between them and dislodge it firmly.

But they'd done it, and Anne sent the video on to Lili. Looks like a horse might be in her future...or at least a riding stable that offers lessons. I'll check it out.

Lili sent a short text back a few minutes later. Something to think about. And great for building responsibility. Video rocked. I miss her like crazy, but she's doing great. Thank you both! Can't wait to see you all when I'm back home.

Anne smiled again.

They didn't want to spoil Addie—that would be easy with three doting adults—but they did want her well-rounded and happy, and if polishing equestrian skills could do that, Anne put her vote firmly in the yes column.

The house was quiet.

Too quiet.

After the confrontation with Tula today, she longed for someone to talk to. Shirley and Regina were at Wednesday night services, Evelyn was at a neighbor's barbecue, and Joy was with her daughter Sabrina's beautiful family. And Ralph was at the hospital.

She was about to feel sorry for herself when he called. "Anne, do you have time to run down here? There's a patient asking for you."

For her?

Anne was surprised, but if this was one of those times when God put her on someone's heart, she wasn't about to mess with it. "Be there in twenty." She drove to the hospital and parked in the parking garage. Ralph would have parked in the Meeting Street lot. The long days of summer kept folks moving, even if it was from one cooled location to another. The air lay thick with moisture and smells, but the city was alive and vibrant with tourists and locals taking advantage of the longer days. She took just a moment to smell the salt water from the bay and make a mental note that she'd pack a lunch and kidnap Ralph for a picnic near the water one of these days.

She texted Ralph once she went through the main entrance doors. WHERE ARE YOU?

ARABELLA.

The beautiful birthing center had been added on to the hospital nearly twenty years before. She walked through the vintage wing, took the exit, then turned in to the separate entrance for the Arabella Cameron Center for Life. The guard waved her through, and she found Ralph to the left of the brightly lit nurses' station. The wings fanned out like pinwheel petals, with each wing having five birthing units. The special care and regular nurseries were straight back, equidistant from the mothers, but the NICU and surgical NICU were to the far right. A generous donation from a local family who'd made their fortunes in shipping had provided funds to make this birthing center unique.

But Ralph wasn't over there, where babies fought to grow and thrive.

He was on the left, near labor and delivery, and the sadness on his face told the story. "A young woman was asking for you. Mariliese. She said she met you the other day."

The young woman being discharged from children's who wasn't ill… She was pregnant. And not nearly far enough along to warrant labor and delivery, a heartbreaking situation.

Anne slipped on a gown and mask before tapping on the closed door down the first wing. "Mariliese?"

"You came." Mariliese reached out a hand when she spotted Anne. Tear-stained cheeks underscored the hard time she was going through. "I remembered your name from your tag, and I asked them to find you. And they did."

Anne crossed the room.

No one else was here.

No father.

No mother.

Just this teenage girl, laboring alone, and scared. So scared. "Of course I came, the minute I heard. Mariliese, where are your parents? Do they know you're here? Do they know what's going on?" Anne slid a chair closer to the bed so she could hold the girl's hand.

"I couldn't get hold of my dad. His phone probably died. He needs a new battery. And Mom—"

Mariliese's chin quivered. Her lower lip thrust out slightly. Tears spilled over her cheeks. Anne handed her a clutch of tissues as her heart went tight. "Does your mom know you're here?"

"She knows." A grimace said more. "She didn't want to come. My friend drove me in when I started bleeding."

Oh, this poor, sweet child. "You know one of my favorite Bible passages is when a woman literally crawls through the crowd to get close to Jesus because she's been bleeding for so long," she said. "No one helps her or acknowledges her, but she finally gets close enough to touch the hem of His garment. Just the hem, mind you. And she's healed. He feels the power go out of Him, and when He realizes it's her, He says 'your faith has healed you.'"

"And did it? For real?" asked Mariliese, but she had to choke the words out around sobs. It broke Anne's heart to see it.

"It did. It's in three separate Gospels—Matthew, Mark, and Luke— the very same story. God knows us, Mariliese. And He loves us."

A pain took hold of the girl then, and when it subsided, she laid her head back against the pillow. "He can't make it," she whispered.

Anne understood that she meant the baby. "I know."

"Only it's weird, you know?" Tears slipped unabashedly again, a mother's tears. "I only just found out about him a few days ago, but the thought of losing him…. Of him dying—" Her breath caught. "I feel like I can't stand it. Like my heart is breaking. How can it be like that when I didn't even know I was pregnant? How can I love him this much?"

"Because you're a mother." A new voice surprised them both. Anne turned as Mariliese's mother slipped into the room. "And mothers will do anything to save their babies, honey. Because we never stop loving them."

Anne stood up and moved to the side.

Mariliese's mother slid into her place—her rightful place—and wrapped her daughter in her arms with soothing words, laced with love.

As Anne moved to the door, Mariliese's mother called her name.

Anne paused.

"Thank you." She mouthed the words so that Anne could see them, and as Anne went through the door, the harried father hurried past her, not seeing her, with eyes only for his child. His daughter.

As it should be.

A room of heartbreak. Of sorrow. But hope too, that a family torn asunder could be brought together again.

"Well." Ralph slung an arm around Anne's shoulders and pulled her close. "You're amazing, Anne Mabry."

They moved toward the shadow of the nursery, a small corner of privacy while Anne wiped her eyes and blew her nose.

"You touched her heart in an elevator ride and she didn't forget it, but then again, I'm not surprised, because you won my heart on the steps of McCutchen House over forty years ago, and you've held it ever since."

"Ralph." She smiled through her tears as she remembered that day when they were both seniors at USC. She swiped her eyes once more. "You couldn't have known. It's not possible."

He grinned and said what he always said when she pooh-poohed his idea of love at first sight. "With God, all things are possible. Just because it took you a while..."

"It did," she answered, laughing, because he'd come on a little strong and Anne wasn't about to be steamrolled in love or life, even back then. "But then I realized that I never wanted a speck of life without you, so I caved."

"And made me the happiest man on earth," he said. He took a breath and stepped back. "I'm going to stay until this is over. I'm glad her parents are here. Seeing her alone reminded me of what happened with Lili and how we let things get fractured when we should have known better. But then we fixed it, and maybe it's made us better for things like this." He indicated Mariliese's room with a glance. "Not stronger, maybe. But wiser."

"I'll have supper waiting."

"That sounds great."

She left the building, knowing Mariliese was in good hands. The right hands. Somehow her mother had conquered anger and embarrassment to come to her daughter's side in her time of need, and that was a huge step forward.

Losing a baby or a child was hard. So hard.

But love and faith could help. Anne knew that. She'd pray that Mariliese and her family found the truth in that too.

Shifting Winds Home for Erring Women

December 1894

A sharp, hurried knock interrupted the morning baking of bread. Helen crossed the room as Colleen rolled out the next loaf. When Helen opened the door, Maisy's oldest daughter stood on the stoop. She opened her mouth then spotted Colleen. Her throat convulsed, and she darted a quick look from Colleen to Helen.

"Annie, good morning!" Helen gave her a bright smile and bid her in by stepping back and waving a hand. "So nice to see you. Your mama said you might be stopping by, so I expect you're in need of a hand with that project?" She spoke with warmth as if it were any old day, but she'd been warned by Maisy that if Annie or Dahlia appeared, Augustina's time had come, and this was over a full month early.

"Yes, ma'am, and if you're too busy—"

"Colleen will finish the bread, and we've a quiet day here so far. Give me a few minutes to gather my cape and gloves. If you head back home, I'll follow right along."

Annie nodded, evidently understanding what couldn't be said out loud. "Thank you." She slipped out the door and after it shut snugly behind her, Helen left to retrieve her long cape, scarf, and gloves from the front closet. She'd packed what she might need in her shopping bag, the bag she toted through the market areas regularly. She came back through and caught Colleen's eye as she stuffed a few extra supplies beneath her cape. "I'll be careful, my friend."

"You have to be. Freedom doesn't always mean equality. If folks find out you're helping bring a Black baby into the world, there are some who will take exception."

"A baby's a baby, Colleen."

Colleen looked unconvinced. "Not to some."

"There will always be 'some.'" Helen put a gentle hand on her coworker and friend's arm. "These hands were made to help as needed. Look how well Clara Barton did last year with her work after that horrible storm. She helped every-one who needed it, with no exceptions."

"Well, she was able to pack her bags and go back home when it was all said and done," Colleen whispered. "She doesn't live here and run a home that's already got a target on its back, Helen."

There was truth in Colleen's words, but it wasn't a truth Helen could abide by. God's truth won out. "I'll be careful."

Colleen grimaced but nodded. She knew it would do no good to argue, but Helen understood her concerns. There had been stern disapproval of Shifting Winds from the beginning, as if showing kindness to laboring women was an affront.

But she could never regret her choice, and when she delivered a tiny, squalling baby boy less than three hours later, she was overcome with joy even though the wee fellow was premature, and would need special care to survive. She'd have to school Tina and her family on how that was done. For the moment, she tucked the baby alongside his mother's body with strict instruction. "You can't have him take a chill. Keep him tucked inside your clothes. Your body warmth will keep him warm, Tina. Just a diaper and nothing else, all right? A chill for a baby born too soon can be their undoing. He cries well. That's a good sign. A slight cry often means weak lungs, and healthy lungs are essential."

Tina looked scared. Maybe this turn of events would grow the willful child up as her mother hoped.

"I'll stay and help," said Dahlia. "I have the time, and that way Mama and Annie can keep working. Estelle gets too nervous around babies. I don't think we need her practicing her untried skills on little Abram."

Helen had known Maisy's family for years, and she knew Estelle. Instinct told her that the young married woman stayed shy of babies for a different reason. She'd been married for over three years with no sign of a family yet, but if Estelle didn't want to talk about it, Helen hesitated to broach the topic.

She finished gathering things for washing as she approached the next dangerous topic. Once she'd put the bundle of bedding into a basket and washed her hands in the basin of clean, soapy water Annie had fetched, she perched on the edge of the bed and locked eyes with Augustina. "And now we must speak of something else." She took a breath because the delicacy of the subject was understood in South Carolina. "This is a white man's child, Augustina."

The girl swallowed hard and looked away. Mouths agape, Annie and Dahlia drew closer, perhaps understanding the import of Helen's questioning.

"Tina, did this man force himself on you?" She knew it happened all too often.

Tina shook her head, and Helen breathed a sigh of relief.

Tina's hands fisted. Tears slipped down her cheeks. Bearing a child out of wedlock was poorly looked on but not necessarily an unforgiveable sin in society's eyes. But for a Black woman to bear a white man's child branded her and her entire family for judgment and condemnation, regardless of whether she had been violated or not.

"Tina." Annie didn't scold. She bent low and took her sister into a gentle hug, but Dahlia had enough scolding for both of them.

"You don't think," she exclaimed hotly. "About others, about family, about anything but your sorry self." She folded her arms and stared hard at her sister. "What are we going to do with a white child here, Tina? What kind of life have you brought this child into? And you know it is against the law to have anything personal to do with a white man, and yet you put not just you but this child and

our whole family in danger for your own personal pleasure. What an unbelievably selfish thing to do."

Tina cried harder.

"This won't help matters." Helen spoke calmly, but her
brain spun, looking for answers at a time when answers
didn't come easy. "Your mother is light-skinned."

"As is Estelle," agreed Annie. "But if that child remains
as pale as he is now, Miss Davis, there ain't a soul here-
abouts who won't know that he's a white man's child, and
you know what kind of torment that can rain down on all
of us. There are rules, written and unwritten, and the
Lord Himself knows the evil that befalls those who break
those rules of separation."

She was right. Abram's lighter skin would have folks
talking. And then acting. And therein lay the danger.

"We send them north," declared Dahlia. "People there
are likely more accepting."

"Send me away?" Eyes wide, Tina met her sister's gaze.
Knowing the youngest sister's lack of work ethic, Helen
couldn't see that turning out very well.

And then Estelle walked into the room. Estelle, a stout
woman, the only stout one of the sisters. A quiet, kind
woman who shied away from limelight, married to a similar man.

A darker-skinned man, but Estelle and Maisy took
the honey-toned coloring from some white ancestor, no
doubt, and—

Did Helen dare make a suggestion?

Deciding she couldn't live with herself if she didn't, Helen crossed to Estelle's side and took her hands. "He's tiny, but he's here, and he looks like you, Estelle. Like you and Tina." Both sisters bore a resemblance to their mother although their coloring varied. Tina was darker skinned, like her father. Estelle was pale by comparison. "He's going to need someone."

Estelle's eyes shot to hers. They went wide, then narrow. "I don't know what you mean."

Helen leaned in and whispered softly, "You do, sweet thing. I see your eyes go to Dahlia's baby when she's not looking. And how you drink up Annie's little Buttercup like she were your own, such a blessed, sweet child." She pulled back and met Estelle's gaze. "A first child often comes early, and he would have a respectable home with two parents. Something to talk with Troy about, perhaps?" She didn't press too hard. Planting a seed of solution was better accomplished with a gentle hand. Not all men favored the raising of someone else's child, and this little guy had a tough enough start. Better to take time and make it right.

Estelle moved forward.

Tina had stopped sobbing, but the tears still flowed, as if finally realizing the far-reaching effects of her choices. Not just on her and her devout family but on this innocent baby.

Estelle perched a hip on the edge of the narrow bed. "May I see him?"

Tina edged the blanket away from the wee boy's head. She picked him up and he curled against her chest, one hand fisted against his mouth and wavy dark hair framing a tiny face.

Estelle touched one of his curls. "Will he make it?"

"I don't know." Helen spoke the truth. "I've yet to lose a baby, but he's not even five pounds. There's much that can go wrong, but if he stays next to Tina for a few weeks, gaining strength and eating, being kept warm, it's possible." Maisy's house wasn't cold, but it wasn't warm either, and the next six weeks would be cold, dank, even this far south. "I'm hoping he'll do fine."

And then Tina did something Helen had rarely seen in the girl.

She reached out a hand to Estelle. "I know you said you don't like babies all that much."

Estelle flushed.

"But I also know that's because you don't have one, Stelle. I heard you crying one night and Troy telling you it would be all right, even if it was always just you two."

Annie reacted in surprise. So did Dahlia.

Tears welled in Estelle's eyes. "No one was supposed to hear those things."

"I know, but I did. Maybe this could work." She leaned down and kissed the tiny newborn's head. "I have made so many mistakes in life, but I don't want him to take the brunt, Stelle. I want him to have a chance." She looked up at her mother. "I'm not saying that we lie to get myself out of trouble."

"Would not be the first time you've done that, child." Maisy folded her arms, and her firm expression meant business.

"I have, but this is not like that. This is for him. Little Abram."

"Abraham."

Three sets of eyes looked at Estelle in surprise.

"If we do this—I must talk with Troy first—but if we do, I like the full name the Lord gave to His servant. It's a name I've always cottoned to if we—"

She didn't finish, but she didn't have to. Helen understood what she meant.

"Abraham is a beautiful name." Annie let that thought dangle in the air, and then Tina sighed.

"It is a beautiful name. And he would have a wonderful mama and daddy. If you're willing."

Helen held her breath.

No one but her and Clara O'Herlihy knew of this dilemma. And Maisy's family, of course. Could it work?

With God's help, yes.

She prayed, and when Estelle stood up she said, "I'll go see Troy at the shop right now." Troy's father and grandfather had been enslaved welders. Troy was born into freedom, and the business the two older men forged was his legacy. He himself had become a master welder at a young age. Would he accept this child? Could he?

Time would tell.

She gave Annie and Dahlia a set of instructions, then Dahlia followed her downstairs. "I'm going to work for the reverend for a week or so," she told Helen. "Mama would never lie to him, so she asked him for a week or two off and he said yes, of course. For a man who does things proper, he has a blessed tolerance for those who make mistakes, doesn't he?"

"He does." In a time when some preachers embraced fire and brimstone, Robert spoke of tolerance, forgiveness, and love. And many folks listened.

"As do you," Dahlia said. "If I'm at the rectory then Mama can be here making sure things are as best as they can be. And if Estelle and Troy take Abraham—"

"Pretending he's theirs."

Dahlia winced, then shrugged. "An adopted child becomes the parents' own. Save for some legalities, that's what we're doing. And that's no one's business but ours. The Lord has protected many a woman and child in His time. We are not the first to seek such protection."

Wise words. Deceit wasn't right, but in an unforgiving society, baring one's soul could be disastrous. It was a lesson she shared with many a young mother. "Thank you, Dahlia." Dahlia turned off the walk to go toward the rectory, while Helen took the back paths through the woods and along the river then cut back to the manor once she'd reached its border.

She slipped into the kitchen and hooked her cape and scarf as Colleen came in the other way. "All is well?" she asked as Helen lay her gloves along the heat grate to dry.

"Yes."

"Helen." Colleen moved forward, troubled. "You risk much to help people outside our circle, and our circle is troubled enough, isn't it? My sympathies lie with these women, but—"

"Our sympathies must lie with all women." Helen wouldn't let her go further. She understood the possible banishment if people realized she was helping Black mothers. She was already skating a thin line of acceptance by helping unwed mothers. "But I shall be discreet, because you're right. There is much to lose. But with every baby we help, Colleen, there is so much more to gain."

Chapter Fourteen

"THAT'S HIM!" JOY HAD BEEN slugging an iced coffee, and when Cabbie Joe Brown trotted down the parking garage steps, she set the cup on Anne's hood and headed toward him. Anne clicked the lock, then followed.

He made a sharp left when he spotted them coming his way.

Anne wasn't about to let him get away, and she'd worn her best weapon: running shoes. She cut to her right quickly and was in his path before he realized she was coming. When Joy pulled up to a stop alongside her, he started to go around them but paused when Anne spoke up. "Joe Brown? Abel Jackson's friend, now known as Cabbie Joe the DJ?"

"Former friend. The guy's a rat, and I should have known that a long time ago, lady, so if you don't mind, please get out of my way. Some of us have jobs." He gave them an insolent look.

"But your job doesn't pay you enough to afford rent, so you bunk in Wellington Manor?" asked Anne outright.

He'd started to turn away.

He stopped and swung back. Then a light of recognition came into his eyes. "You were at the house the other day."

"As were you."

"Abel said it was all right."

"Abel the rat?"

He frowned. "He is a rat, but he also knows I helped him when I could. He was cheated out of his inheritance by a rich granddaddy who never saw his worth, and now who has the last laugh?" He smirked. "Byron ended up with nothing, Abe cornered the app market and could buy and sell his goody-two-shoes cousin multiple times, and I ended up owing medical fees for my son's illness. Fees that took my house and my wife, but that's my sob story. Not yours. Why are you haranguing me?"

"Did you kill Byron Wellington?"

Pure surprise hiked the man's brows. "He's dead?"

Anne refused to show a reaction. "That's not an answer."

"I haven't seen or heard from Byron for thirty years, not since the world blew up over those two little kids that died and the world sided with their parents. Now there's a put-up job if ever I saw one. Nobody ever pointed a finger at the parents for having those boys riding in the back seat, facing the rear, even though there was room for them in the middle seat with their sister. The mother said they liked it back there, that they were quieter when they were together and not pestering their sister," he went on, as if a dam had just burst within him.

"Why didn't anyone call the parents out for that? Any parent knows that the safest place for kids is the middle seat in a wagon. What kind of person puts their kids in the back on a superhighway because they're too noisy to be in the middle? Not the kind I am," he finished. And then he blew out a breath, a long one. "Sorry." He waved a hand over his face to cool himself off, but that gesture wasn't going to help in today's heat and humidity. "I don't talk about that much, and it's probably good that I don't, because Byron got rail-roaded over that whole thing. And that never should have happened. Stupid parents annoy me."

"Do you just have the one son, Joe?" Anne asked.

"Two kids. A boy and a girl. They live with my ex-wife in my ex-house, and I pay child support by living in Byron's den."

"And is your boy going to be all right? The one who was sick?"

He sighed. "Yes, thank God. He's going to be fine."

"And the missing items from Wellington Manor?" Joy led him with the question.

He frowned. "I don't know what you're talking about. I've never taken anything from anyone. Not my gig. But I knew that Byron wouldn't care if I stayed there. Not if he knew the circumstances. Why it's sitting empty and alone is beyond me, but hey." He shrugged. "The price is right."

"There are a lot of folks who are one trauma away from home-lessness," said Anne, and he acknowledged that with a nod.

"Never thought it would be me, but it is, and you're right. But as long as my kids are okay, and they're happy, nothing else matters. They're fourteen and sixteen. I married later than most my age, and they keep me young."

"Tell me about Byron."

Anne's question made a crease in his forehead. "Why should I?"

"Because if you're innocent then you should want him to lay claim to that house. It's going to revert to the preservation society in just a few weeks if we don't find Byron and give him the chance to know this. Unless he's no longer with us." Anne added that last sentence with a pointed expression.

Cabbie Joe swiped his sleeve to his brow. "I've never done anything to anyone, nor would I, but it's ninety-one degrees and the air is pea-soup thick. Can we take this somewhere else?"

"Can we buy you lunch?" queried Joy.

Anne agreed quickly. A guy living in an empty house might benefit from a decent meal. "Sena Café?" The highly regarded café wasn't far away, and their delectable food made it an easy choice.

"You don't mind?"

The question gave Anne a better insight into Cabbie Joe's persona. He didn't want to be homeless. Nor did he want to be a drain on society, but when death or divorce splits an income, fallout was often inevitable. "Of course not. Can we give you a lift?"

"That would be great."

When they got to the cozy Mt. Pleasant restaurant, Anne let food bridge the initial gap. Her mother had always said that food was a basic equalizer, and no one argued with Mama.

It worked.

When Joe had plowed through a prime rib and swiss sandwich, a bowl of soup, and two cups of coffee, she knew the time was right. "Where is Byron, Joe? Or where do you think he is?"

Joe sighed. "Well, that's the question, isn't it? Two of the cousins tried to find him way back when, and I know Abe's tried a couple of other times. He's not really a rat," Joe continued, referencing his earlier statement about his old friend. "But he has gotten mighty self-centered. Having so much money that tens of thousands of dollars is pocket change changes a person. And he was really mad that he made his fortunes after his grandfather died."

"That's kind of harsh," said Joy.

"Yes and no," Joe replied. "His grandfather was old school in a new age. He didn't think Abe would amount to anything because Abe went his own way. He dropped out of college, started a software design business in his parents' basement, and was pretty unsuccessful for several years. What Granddad didn't know was that Abel was saving every penny he didn't spend on rent to finance his start-up. He saw things differently," Joe explained. "Abe didn't see the 'whys' of things that would happen, he saw the 'what-ifs,' so when the internet became a thing and cell phones were just getting hot, he saw a way to bridge the gap between access and availability. Those original apps were the cornerstone of his work. And they launched him big-time. There were nights when he threatened to dig his grandpa up to show him what he'd done."

"A 'how do you like me now?' attitude." Anne forked another bite of delicious baklava.

"Yes." Joe nodded. "Exactly like that. Since his grandfather died, nothing's ever been enough for Abe. It's like there's a void, a hollowness that makes no sense to me, because that money opens doors. It could help so many people. Anyway, I went to see him, and I was telling him that, and he pretty much tossed me out. Made me feel like a beggar." The crease between Joe's eyebrows deepened again. "I don't beg. I don't take. I get by, and I may have fallen down on my luck for the time being, but that's a temporary setback. It's not like I don't have a plan, I always have a plan, but sometimes the plans run amok and then you zig when you thought you'd zag."

"You talk like a writer." Joy took a sip of water, watching him.

"I've dabbled. More now that I'm huddled in the den on my own," he confessed. "But it's just scribblings. What I'd really like to do is figure out a way to help folks like me, and that's what Abe didn't understand the last time we met up." He took a swig of coffee. "He keeps a waterfront house on Johns worth a couple of million."

Johns Island was south of the city and home to a real mix of people.

"He calls it a 'stop by' place so he doesn't have to deal with people when he comes to town. A year-round caretaker with a house on the grounds keeps everything ready. Like an old English lord, you know?"

"Austen friendly," declared Anne, and Joe smiled.

"Exactly."

Johns Island had its share of affluent people and gorgeous homes. And regular folks too.

"I didn't schedule the appointment with Abe because I was looking for a personal handout," Joe continued. "I wanted him to finance a way to help others, and I'd help work it because I learned the hard way that folks are often one paycheck away from homelessness and poverty."

"It didn't go well."

"An understatement." Joe took another long gulp of coffee. A waitress came by and refilled his cup. He smiled his thanks, then brought his attention back to Joy and Anne. "As long as my kids don't suffer, it's all right. Nothing's more important than them." He hunched forward. "You asked about Byron. He's not a pain in the neck like Abe. He's more sensitive. Always was. I often wondered if the whole accident thing tipped him over the edge back then. Abe and I were younger. Byron is the oldest grandchild, and he was the beacon their grandpa used to hold up for the others. 'Byron did this, Byron did that.' University of Georgia, then Columbia Medical, then a stint volunteering overseas, doing surgeries that people wouldn't get otherwise, and then back to the Bronx during the worst times there. It was like a war zone back then.

"People said he honed his surgical skills there, with so many trauma patients. It's not like that now," he added. "But it was then. He scored a job in a brand-new hospital they'd just built, and he saved all kinds of lives because he was that special. That good. Even Abe couldn't hold that against him, because Byron didn't care about praise. He just cared about helping people. But Abe said it got to Byron after a while. He got to where he thought he should be able to fix everything." Joe's face turned thoughtful. "And he did, he fixed bodies, so many people, but it was a never-ending stream. Every night, every day. Abe's sister used to pester him to come back to Charleston. Work here. Come home. She worried about him, and eventually he did come back. But she said he was different."

Joy arched her brows in a quiet question.

"As if he wondered what it was all for."

"You're right," said Anne.

He looked at her, surprised.

"I worked in the hospital then. I saw him and heard about the amazing things he'd done and was doing at Mercy. The hospital thought it had scored a coup to get him, but I saw that sadness. As if he'd seen too much."

"Maybe he had." Joe frowned. "And then maybe the lawsuit and all that came with it pushed him over the edge. It can do that to folks, even if they're not overly sensitive. Sometimes life weighs hard, and I always wondered if it got too hard for Byron and maybe he—" He breathed deeply. "Just couldn't take it anymore and did something drastic."

The thought of the skilled doctor taking his own life had crossed Anne's mind too.

"That's when my faith bolsters me," Joy said. "I've spent decades in Houston, helping here, there, and the other place, and it's helped me to be stronger and more sympathetic. It's not easy for a rich person like Abel to empathize with the poor. It's too easy to take credit for what we've done, when sometimes we're just in the right place at the right time or—" She smiled. "We marry the right person. In any case, your Byron sounds like good people to me, Joe. And so do you. We want to find out what happened to him, no matter where the story takes us. In the end, it's better to know."

His phone pinged, and he hit a button. "I've got to go. Missy's got a dentist appointment this afternoon, and I said I'd get her to it."

"But you don't have a car."

"I'll meet her at home, and we'll take the bus. It's a bit of a walk, but that gives us time together."

"Well, let us get you over there," Joy offered. "We've got to go back to the city anyway."

"That would save me a lot of time."

"And Joe, I want to keep you apprised of what we find," Anne told him. "Can I get your contact information?"

He agreed and rattled off his cell number. They dropped him off at a bus stop not far from the bridge, then Anne looked at Joy. "Do you think Abel's in town?"

"One way to find out," Joy replied. "Let's go to the island!"

It wasn't hard to find Abel's place on the water, but the massive driveway gate was a major impediment for the car.

Anne pulled the SUV to the side of the road, tucked her purse up on her shoulder, and stepped out. "Ready for a walk?"

"Yes, ma'am." Joy did the same with her tiny purse.

While the thickly barred wrought iron gate blocked the driveway, there was no wall around the rest of the multimillion dollar property. "Clearly he's only worried about keeping things out that arrive in vehicles," muttered Anne as they wound their way through a grassy area rimmed with trees. The thick trees left the house fairly invisible until they turned a corner, and there it was.

It wasn't opulent.

It was simple and gracious, modeled after New England shore homes, low country friendly. Dormer windows provided a view for the third story, and a wraparound porch spanned the east, south, and west sides. Rockers sat empty on the porch, with small tables in between. It looked like a page out of *Southern Living* magazine, the gorgeous porch overlooking the waters of the Bohicket River. It was a pastoral site until the peaceful moment was broken by a blaring shriek.

"Intruder! Intruder! Intruder!"

Anne's heart raced.

She looked at Joy.

Joy looked back.

And they both ran *to* the house, not away. Anne considered that a victory for womankind. She marched up the side steps, rang the doorbell, then rapped sharply on the door, all while the pesky electronic voice blared the single word pronouncement.

The door swung open, but it wasn't the fiftyish balding man standing tall in the doorway that got Anne's attention.

It was the gun.

Anne swallowed hard. Real hard. *Ralph will never forgive me if I die here today.*

That was what ran through her head. What came out of her mouth, since she was still alive, was something quite different. "For heaven's sake, put the gun away. You're being ridiculous. We've come here on important business, Mr. Jackson, and we're not leaving until it's been accomplished, so there's really no need to shoot us. And besides that, there are people who will stop at nothing to find our bodies."

Abel Jackson eyed the river, then the women, with a doubtful look. "Mighty deep river."

"Really?" Joy tapped her foot, and when Joy tapped her foot, people tended to listen. It was a neat trick that Anne couldn't master. "We're here to talk about Byron. We can talk here"—she indicated the porch with a lift of her chin—"or there." She shifted her attention to the attractive house. "And a proper Southern gentleman would offer folks a glass of sweet tea. I can't believe that a wealthy businessman like yourself wouldn't know that."

He sighed. "I was supposed to be on my way to Europe right now." He frowned. "But the CEO there came down sick, so I'm here, and so are you."

"God's plan!" announced Anne brightly.

"Coincidence," he corrected her, "but I got where I am by never taking a coincidence for granted, so I won't start today. And why are we talking about Byron? That's an old subject and a sore one, to boot."

"Are we coming in?" demanded Joy. "You have a really nice view, but it's hot out here."

He stepped back.

The women walked in. Joy turned around and faced him right away. "This is charming, Mr. Jackson."

"The house sitter does it. Decks it out. Cleans it. I just show up and stay until I leave."

"An itinerant life?" Anne didn't wait to be asked. She moved toward the comfortably appointed living room and took a seat. "I expect that suits a man who's made his fortune in technology. A modern man with modern thoughts."

Her words seemed to make him think. Then he shrugged. "Not the life I expected. But I'll take it."

"Homes worth millions across the globe, innovative patents, an amassed fortune, and a freebird lifestyle," said Joy.

He sat and regarded them with a wry expression. "Is this where you try to convert me or go all inspirational movie on me and convince me to give up my playboy ways and settle down with a nice hometown girl and raise a couple of perfect, photogenic children?"

"Well, I love my faith, so I'm not opposed to option one," Anne told him, "but I'm leaving your personal life right where it should be. With you. We had a chat with Joe Brown earlier."

A shadow darkened his face. "And he told you I'm a jerk."

He was close, but Anne feigned surprise. "No, he actually told us that your grandfather was so stuck in the past that he didn't realize what a talented innovator you were and are. And that it was hard to have Byron held up as an example of the only road to success. If we're measuring success in dollars," she finished.

"There's really no other way, is there?" His cryptic tone suggested he'd had lots of practice being cynical. "Unless we come back to the Hallmark movie scenario. Spare me that."

"Joe said you tried to find Byron."

That got a reaction. He frowned. "Twice. Dead ends both times. I wanted to find him," he added, as if needing to convince them. "But it was like he walked off the face of the earth, and that made it even worse, because what if that's what happened?" He sighed. "What if the whole thing blowing up here in Charleston just tipped him over the edge, and he ended it all? I don't know any other way he could have just disappeared like that."

He shrugged. "What Byron did mattered. It mattered to people. To families. It saved lives. All he ever wanted was to heal the sick, and he got shafted for his efforts. My grandma researched family history long before you could do it online. She liked to equate Byron with the old Dr. Wellington, the one who turned the manor into a home for unwed mothers when his wife died. Tenderhearted, she called him, and she said the same thing about Byron. But maybe there's only so much a tender heart can take, and that made me want to find him. Make peace with him. I was making boatloads of money because I developed software that lets people connect in a virtual way. Byron saved real lives in a very personal way, and I wanted him to know how much I admire that."

"Because you never told him when he was around?"

His grimace said Anne was correct. "I was stupid and young then. Somewhere along the way I grew up. Mostly."

"But your searches found nothing we can follow up on?" asked Joy.

"Nothing. And I hired some big guns. They said it was rare for someone to be so well-hidden that nothing could track them, and that generally, in those cases, the person was no longer with us."

Both Joe and Abel had alluded to sensitivity and suicide. Anne hated to probe but felt like she needed to. "Do you think your cousin took his own life?"

"No. He loved life too much to do that. I think he walked away from all the pettiness and scandal and headbutting that went on at Mercy Hospital back then. My hired guys uncovered some really nasty stuff leading up to Byron's disappearance. How the chief trauma surgeon set up that whole dressing down so that patients would overhear, figuring someone would go to the press with it, and he was right."

"He did that purposely?" Joy didn't hide her surprise. "How do they know that?"

"Because one of the other surgeons told them. It had weighed on his conscience for a decade. When the private investigative team interviewed him, he confessed the whole thing. No laws were broken, there was nothing we could do, but it was despicable. And yet it happens all the time. One colleague will undermine another to gain advantage, but I wouldn't have expected it in medicine."

"It's better now," Anne told him. "I was there then, and some of the doctors resented new blood. Byron was brought on board with all that skill and knowledge and practical experience, and the administration made a big deal of it. He showed up some people who don't like to get shown up."

"Egos." He sighed and splayed his hands. "Byron didn't have an ego. In retrospect I think that was rare for an accomplished surgeon. But he had the biggest heart known to man, so if you find him, and I hope you do, I'm going to be first in line to shake his hand. And then hug him. He was always a little better than anyone else I knew, a little kinder. More focused. And I'd like nothing more than to tell him that. Did Joe Brown tell you I was here?"

Anne shook her head as she stood. "He mentioned he'd come to you with an idea." She didn't say more than that. Abel knew how the meeting had gone down. He was part of it.

His forehead creased slightly as Joy stood too. "We didn't realize you were even in town until he mentioned that, so we took a chance. And here you are."

"Here I am."

The women crossed to the door, and Abel followed them onto the porch. Anne turned before they moved to the steps. "Thank you for seeing us. We appreciate everything you said, Mr. Jackson."

"Abe. Please."

She smiled. So did Joy. "If you think of anything else, let us know." Joy put her name and number on a Post-it note. She generally kept a collection of tiny things in her small purses, and the Post-it notes had come in handy before. "And pray for us to find him."

Her request seemed to startle him, but then a thoughtful expression softened his gaze. He didn't say he would, and he didn't say he wouldn't, but the eased expression indicated he just might. That in itself held hope.

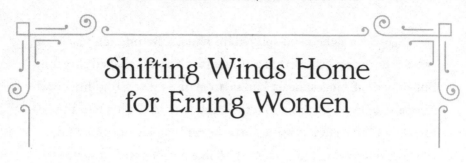

Shifting Winds Home for Erring Women

March 1904

"What an excitement, to have your beautiful daughter getting married!" Clara exclaimed as she helped tote things into the home's kitchen on a bright autumn morning with just enough decrease in temperature and humidity to make one's breath not quite so tight. "Jonathan Brightly is quite a catch in Charleston circles. And won't Miriam be a lovely bride?"

Her precious girl, a bride. Helen pushed aside the knot in her throat. "She certainly will."

"And officiated by the reverend who's known her for so many years."

Clara's enthusiasm drove a stab of guilt into Helen. It was one thing to live a quiet life side by side as if all was normal and well. She and Robert had done much good by working together, but the thought of sitting at a formal event as mother of the bride while Robert performed the faith-filled ceremony nearly made her swoon. Why was that, after so many years?

The thought left her weak-kneed, and yet there were no other options. It would be an insult to St. Andrew's and

Robert to have Miri's wedding any other place, and Miri herself wouldn't hear of such a thing. But of course, she knew nothing. Nor would she. Ever.

"She was eight years old when you came here to run Shifting Winds. Helen, can you believe it's been almost sixteen years?"

"We've helped a lot of women, Clara."

"More you and Robert than anyone, dear Helen. I know it doesn't set well with all, but I am so impressed by both of you. You have put faith in action, not just word, and isn't that the grandest thing? You've given folks a second chance, and at great personal sacrifice."

Helen swallowed hard, surprised. She turned toward Clara then breathed easier when Clara added, "To stay widowed and not even entertain the thought of another man, to focus your attention on the child God gave you and your mission here. Helen, I have so much respect for you."

She'd written her turmoil in her journals. She'd laid the story out for all to see someday, but the thought of people respecting her for living a lie weighed on her now.

It hadn't before. She justified it as a sin forgiven, and it was, but as the years went on, her own part in it sat like a stone in her chest.

"Are you all right?" Clara moved closer. "I have salts. Do you need some?"

"I'm fine." Helen sank onto a stone bench outside the kitchen. In two weeks they would celebrate her daughter's wedding and proclaim their faith and belief before God, something she did all the time. Why, then, did this loom different?

Because it was Miriam. Her blessed daughter. Fruit of her womb.

"I'm going to take these tomatoes home for canning," Clara told her. "Then I'll have Simon bring them back for your larder here. A bountiful garden and a beautiful bride. Praise be!"

Colleen poked her head out the kitchen door after Clara left. She took one look at Helen, swiped her hands to her apron, and came forward. She took a seat alongside Helen and quietly folded her hands. Eyes down, she sat quiet, not saying a word.

"I'm unsure of myself, Colleen."

"I see that," her friend replied.

"I look around at the beauty surrounding me, at the grace of the life I've lived here—"

"The good we've done."

She made a wry face. "Or perhaps the good done to us by the grace of giving. It is always better to give than to receive."

"You're beating yourself up, Helen. Don't."

Helen faced her friend and for the first time addressed the topic that had hung by a thread between them for years, still unacknowledged. "You know the truth."

"I have suspected," Colleen corrected her. "And not by any untoward look or action but by silence. You've made it so far with peace, to have it unravel now with Miri's wedding coming up would be awful. And yet, I see the unrest in you."

"To understand living a lie, one must have lived a lie."

"No." Colleen argued. She took Helen's hands firmly. "To make the best of a bad situation is a good thing. Many have done so before you. But I have always wondered, Helen, why you never married. You and Robert, I mean. Why deny yourselves the warmth of love and marriage?"

Helen didn't look at Colleen.

She gazed out over the gardens, unmolested by hurricanes this year. Fruits and vegetables in abundance, canned for winter. Herbs, drying in the kitchen pantry. And half a dozen young pigs being raised for fall slaughter. "I felt it would make the lie worse."

Colleen groaned.

Helen wanted to groan too, because it didn't seem to make sense now, but it seemed to at the time. "Our timing was off from the beginning. When I realized I was with child, Robert had just been given his ministerial assignment at the shore. I could see he would rise to admiration within the church. It was his destiny. And so I left him to pursue his life, and I would pursue mine, a life with a child he knew not of. He married. Rose in prominence, as I expected. And then he lost his wife when the children were small. That loss showed him the pangs and dangers of childbirth. His mission to begin this home had nothing to do with me."

Colleen's eyebrows shifted up. "I didn't realize that. I assumed..."

"That he started Shifting Winds because of my predicament," Helen filled in. "But that wasn't the case. It wasn't until he sought me out to be the midwife here that he realized he had a daughter. A daughter that looks like me but bears his traits. And so it began."

"And you never pursued this relationship because..." Question thickened Colleen's voice.

"Atonement. Vision. Mission?" She clasped one hand with the other, then sighed. "Guilt. His. Mine. I think Shifting Winds loomed as a manner of reparation. A way to wipe the slate clean. I knew that if we pursued a relationship eventually someone would notice a resemblance between Robert and Miriam. Not in her appearance, so much, but her mannerisms. The way she angles her head and arches that eyebrow, so much like him. And her laugh. His laugh. Someone would put it together."

"As I did."

"Yes. And to what end, Colleen? To end his career? To ruin the way he touches hearts and souls with his goodness? And honestly, I have trusted in God's forgiveness all this time, and it has worked, even as Robert struggled. Until now, that is. Now the thought of him officiating her wedding and her not knowing makes my pulse jump. The thought of possible grandchildren denied the chance to love and respect him as they could and should." She lifted her shoulders. "The lie becomes multiplied, and I don't think I can bear that."

"Well, you have to."

Colleen's matter-of-fact voice helped.

"There are no options, dear Helen. None. To come clean now would ruin not just Miri's wedding but her life. People would look at her differently. Instead of being the educated and successful young news reporter who has taken our city by storm with her exposés, she'd be branded. There are restive factions in this city."

Helen knew that. Hadn't she hidden her help for women of color for that very reason?

"Plead your guilt with God, but keep your silence here, my friend." Colleen gave her a half hug. "This is one time when the truth will not set you or her or Robert free. It could, in fact, spell disaster for all three of you. This is a moment and a time to trust in God but not necessarily in man. You know what's been happening lately."

She did know. And Colleen was right. Sometimes silence was best. Which meant the guilt was hers to deal with. She took a deep breath and stood. "I will keep my silence, Colleen."

Colleen didn't try to hide her look of relief.

"You're right. There is so much to lose and little to gain, because God's forgiveness should be enough."

"Amen to that. Come on." She took Helen's hand and started for the house. "I've got lunch ready. Gillian is showing signs that labor is imminent, and you'll need your stamina for she is not exactly the stoic type."

"Then we shall help her become more so. Or stuff cotton in our ears," said Helen, laughing. "As long as we safely deliver her, it will be fine."

And when a squalling, bald, beautiful baby girl was laid in the young mother's arms about nine hours later, the blessing of the newborn's health made it fine indeed.

Chapter Fifteen

CHANGE OF PLANS. CAN'T MEET AT MY PLACE TODAY, HUBBY IS HOSTING BASEBALL NIGHT DUE TO SICK FRIEND. JOY, YOUR PLACE?

Joy read Evelyn's text to Anne as Anne drove past the Angel Oak to intersect the Maybank Highway. The glorious old tree had been featured in stories and legends, and it always made her pause to appreciate life whenever she passed it.

"The café," suggested Anne. "They won't be busy at three thirty, and your brick cleaners are going to be cleaning your place around then, aren't they?"

"Yes, so the café is perfect. Not to mention the option of Bud's amazing sticky buns for supper. I can never eat a full supper after a big lunch." Joy texted Evelyn and Shirley, and by the time they got to Anne's parking spot, they had just enough time to get in a good walk to the coffee shop. Ginger greeted them as they walked in.

"Ladies, perfect timing." Ginger wasn't called that because of her strawberry-blond hair or a shortened form of Virginia. She was named Ginger by her father because he said she was born sassy and deserved a name to match. She pointed to a corner table. "I see Shirley and Evelyn heading this way, so why don't you gals get situated and I'll start your drinks. The usual?"

"Yes please," said Anne. A nod from Joy confirmed Ginger's question. "Do you know all the hospital crew this well?"

"Just my favorites." Ginger winked because everyone was a favorite with her.

"The great coffee is only one reason to love this place," said Joy as she pulled out her phone. "Ginger and Bud make this place shine, don't they?"

"They sure do." Ginger and Bud had started the café a dozen years before. It withstood some tough times, but they'd hung on and now they were listed on so many "places to stop while you're in Charleston" lists that mornings and lunches could be frantically busy during the tourist season. The later afternoons held a welcome lull, and the women were happy to take advantage of it.

Shirley came in the door, followed by Evelyn. They waved to Ginger.

She waved back, and the two women crossed the cozy setting to join Anne and Joy. Evelyn's pencil had gone askew in her hair. She wound it back in snugly and launched right in. "I'm not sure why I thought tackling that dusty cavern of a room was a good idea, but the interns made great progress today, as did I," she announced. "We should have it looking somewhat normal by next week and fully organized by month's end. And that's something I never thought I'd be able to say this summer."

"The entire hospital administration will thank you for it," said Anne. She winked at Evelyn, who laughed. Anne knew that restoring order to that room was more for Evelyn's peace of mind than anything and that the administration probably had no clue it was even happening.

"Who goes first?" asked Evelyn once Ginger had brought their drinks over. "My news is only about dusting, so I'm a drudge today, but Joy's got a sparkle in her eye, and Shirley can barely sit still in her seat. You first." Evelyn pointed to Joy. "What happened with Cabbie Joe?"

Anne and Joy filled them in. They kept their voices low. Anne had learned a hard lesson earlier in the week, and she didn't want anyone overhearing. With only four occupied tables in the twelve-table café, Anne felt fairly secure. When Anne explained how they followed up with a visit to Abel Jackson, Evelyn whistled softly. "That's gutsy. He's pretty much a hermit, I hear. A couple of Wilson's friends have tried to get to know him over the years, but he's both an infrequent visitor to his house on the river and somewhat antisocial."

"Not abnormal for geeks," said Anne. "It's pretty well known that geeks and engineers tend to think about things differently. Their brains don't work like ours, and what we find amusing, they may find tedious."

"I heard an engineer say that very thing on *Jeopardy!* last year," agreed Joy. "It made me understand some of Wilson's friends better."

"Abe wants his cousin found so he can make amends?"

"Yes. And I'd love to see that happen too." Anne took a long sip of her iced coffee.

"If you ladies are done?" Shirley's eyes sparkled with anticipation as she awaited their confirmation.

"Yes, ma'am," said Anne.

"I believe so," added Joy.

"Well how about this?" Shirley held up a picture on her phone.

"'Graybill Office and Stationery Supply Company.'" Anne read the caption out loud then raised her brows in Shirley's direction.

"Proud producers of preprinted office supplies, including medical prescription pads in the thirties, forties, and fifties." Shirley practically crowed the words.

"They made the prescription papers we found?" Evelyn turned toward Shirley. "And you never said a word on the walk over!"

"I wanted to see the looks on all your faces," drawled Shirley, then she grinned. "And it was worth it. These particular pads were only sold to a few states including Virginia, North Carolina, and South Carolina. I've tracked down a Wellington relative who had a small medical practice up in Greensboro."

"That's not far from Durham, is it?"

"About an hour, give or take, but it seems that Dr. Wellington Clancy Lovell was a frequent visitor to Charleston while he was courting his wife eighty-some years ago. The manor was no longer a home for unwed mothers. There was plenty of space to bunk a relative in need, and Robert Wellington did that often, it seems."

"That puts this Lovell man in the right place..." Anne began.

"The manor," added Joy.

"With possible access to the proper prescription pad," declared Evelyn. "So did he write the verse on the back? And to what does it lead?" she wondered.

"I don't know, but I want another shot at that house," said Anne. "I've got time on Saturday. Addie doesn't come home until Sunday, so we could do a little on-site exploration, couldn't we?"

"If the window's unlocked."

"We could text Cabbie Joe and ask him to be sure to leave it open," suggested Joy. "But what are we looking for?"

"Something that ties in with the prescription pads," said Anne. "If it was a game, then let's figure out how it's played. If it's a series of clues, let's figure them out."

"What if one thing has nothing to do with the other?" Evelyn posed the question with her usual sensibility. "I think anyone with a keepsake box realizes that the things in that box are often individual. A locket that has nothing to do with a letter, a picture that's unrelated to either. Isn't it possible that the only important thing in that box is the will?"

Anne agreed. "I've thought the same thing, but then I ask myself, what if they are related? What if the weird things going on with Wellington Manor and Byron and Lorilyn and Tula are interconnected? Like that game that shows degrees of separation and how everyone is related somehow."

"It could be." This was Joy answering. "But we need to keep an open mind and realize it's got an equal shot at being unrelated too. Like Evelyn, I'm concerned if we waste so much time down a rabbit hole we lose the narrow window of time we do have."

"Should we skip breaking into the empty house then?" asked Anne, and three sets of eyes met her gaze with surprise.

"No." Evelyn made a face. "My pretense of practicality was just that. I can't wait to get back into that house. It's fascinating, and I want to know who's dusting it. Who's watching over it? And why?"

Joy shrugged. "As long as we keep our eye on the prize, I'm all in."

"Me too," said Shirley.

Anne was about to set a time with them when something in her peripheral vision made her pause. It wasn't a person, per se.

More like a shadow.

With no one there to cast it.

Goose bumps prickled her arms and neck. The impossibility of the shadow just beyond the window overlooking the East Bay parking lot wasn't lost on her, but it was there.

She put a finger to her lips. As soon as she attempted to stand, the shadow disappeared.

But did it really? Or did shifting her line of sight change things?

She stood, shoved back her chair, and hurried to the door. She thrust it open.

Nothing was there.

Not on the street. No one to be seen except for small groups of people out and about, a mix of locals and tourists.

Was she seeing things?

"What was it?" Evelyn had come up alongside. "Did you hear something? See something?"

What could she say?

She sighed and shook her head. "I thought I did, but I must have been wrong, because it's absolutely impossible. I thought—"

Right then a figure emerged up the road.

Tula.

Or someone who dressed and walked and looked like Tula.

She darted across the street and disappeared into one of the narrow alleyways leading away from the waterfront.

But there was no way Tula could have been on the sidewalk, casting the shadow Anne saw, and then be down the road. And she did work in the hospital, so walking the streets in this area after her busy workday wasn't unusual.

But Anne's heart beat quickly in her chest. "Is it a coincidence that we're talking at Ginger's and we happen to see Tula up the road?"

"It could be, but I doubt it."

The certainty in Evelyn's voice made Anne feel better.

"Someone is dogging our tails, and she may have followed me and Shirley."

"To what end?" breathed Anne. "Is she that afraid of Schlater?"

"For good reason," Evelyn said. They moved back to the table to finish their drinks, and Anne pitched right into a funny story about her early parsonage days. The other women caught on at once and joined in the new topic of conversation. Once they were outside, Anne filled them in on Tula's appearance.

"You think it was her?" asked Joy. "The shadow, I mean?"

Shirley took a more practical angle. "What was the shadow's orientation?"

Anne frowned. "I don't know what you mean."

"Like where was the head?"

"Oh." Anne moved a few steps down the sidewalk. "Here," she said, and pointed to a spot near the curb. "It was silhouetted on the walk, just briefly, like one of those old locket silhouettes."

Shirley pointed up. "Whoever it was was up there," she told them. "For the sun to cast a shadow like that at this time of day, the person had to be above the sidewalk with the sun to their back. That means they were on one of the upper floors leaning out, or on the roof."

The roof.

Of course!

Anne gripped Shirley's hand. "Tour guides have access to all kinds of odd places. Cemeteries, churches, and buildings. It's possible that Tula was up there, and I never thought about how the shadow was cast. Just that it was there. Oh, bless you, I thought I was losing it for a minute."

"But why is she dogging us?" Shirley frowned. "She might not want us riling up Doc Schlater, but that wouldn't make her spy on us, would it? So what's Tula Manchester got to lose? There's something she isn't telling us, and I expect it's got something to do with that young man who looks a lot like Byron Wellington. I say it's time to track her down and ask those questions. Because if that's Byron's son, maybe Miss Tula knows more than she's letting on."

# Chapter Sixteen

WHAT DID TULA MANCHESTER WANT? Anne wondered the next morning.

And what did she have to lose?

A son? If the young man who resembled Byron was her child, a son she'd managed to hide for decades, was he in danger? Was she protecting that handsome young man?

Anne got into the hospital early, determined to face off with Tula. She took an elevator to the ground level and crossed to the food service kitchens down the corridor to the left. The busy kitchen area wasn't a place she generally saw, and the quick-paced rhythm of the workers charged with getting breakfast up to over three hundred patients was amazing.

She pushed through a swinging door and approached the kitchen manager's area. She didn't want to get Tula in trouble, but she wasn't about to stand down either.

Shakilah motioned her into the small office. She was finishing a phone call, and when she'd disconnected, she faced Anne. "Hey, Anne. How can I help you?"

"I just need a couple of minutes with Tula," Anne explained. "I can come down anytime. I don't want to interrupt her work."

"No problem." Shakilah indicated the door with a thrust of her chin. "She's just gone off to deliver the baked goods. The kiosk in the Angel Wing is her last stop, so if you go over there, you'll catch her in about ten or twelve minutes. After that she's in the cafeteria, overseeing the service line."

Anne thanked her and hurried back to the silver elevators. She could cross over the ground floor and take the stairs up to the Angel Wing, but that would mean walking by the morgue, and Anne had every intention of avoiding that. She knew morgues were a necessity, but she was 100 percent all right with skirting the vicinity.

She got to the coffee kiosk about six minutes later. Two young women worked the busy coffee station, one of several tucked around the hospital and professional building corridors, a huge improvement over the old way of having one big coffee service in the lobby. That one still existed, but the satellite versions meant people got their coffee and snacks quickly and could get back to work.

She waited the six minutes.

No Tula.

Then eight.

Still no Tula.

She waited another five, then decided she was being silly. She knew the general route of kiosks, cafeteria, and coffee shop, so she headed back toward the lobby, sure to meet Tula coming this way.

She was just passing the in-house café when she spotted Tula's cart in an alcove.

She hurried that way. The cart was tucked aside. Not out of sight, but not drawing attention to itself either.

Still no Tula.

Bathroom break?

Anne knew the food carts and coffee services were never supposed to be left unattended and when the minutes stretched on, she became worried. Where was Tula?

She poked her head out of the nook and looked left. Then she looked right.

No Tula.

Her heart began to beat harder. Faster.

Tula Manchester wasn't a park-and-run cupcake service. She was a person who took her job seriously, so what was going on these past two weeks? What was really wrong?

Anne put both hands on the bakery cart and pushed it over to the information desk centered in the beautifully appointed lobby.

"New job, Anne?" joked Polly, another volunteer. "I want that job," she went on, laughing. "Only I'd eat a pastry a day, minimum, and then where would I be? Plumper than I am." She laughed, then looked at Anne's face more closely. "What's up? What's wrong?"

"Tula's cart."

Polly frowned, not understanding.

"It was parked in the nook at the far end, she never got to the Angel Wing, and she hasn't come back for it."

"Sick or indisposed," reasoned Polly. "I expect she'll either come this way from the ladies' room or Food Service will send up a replacement. In any case, I'm going to grab two of those fritters for us." She tucked a five-dollar bill beneath a tray of pastries. "Tell Brenda at the kiosk it's from me."

"I will." Anne wheeled the cart to the Angel Wing. Evelyn spotted her from the records area and came her way.

"You're on cart detail?"

"Tula disappeared."

Evelyn's brows shot up. "What exactly does that mean?"

"If only I knew," Anne replied. "I went downstairs to see her, but she was already making rounds of the coffee stations, so I came over to this one to meet her and she never got here. I wanted to find out why she's been watching us, but she never arrived at this kiosk." She motioned to the mini-café area just beyond the records unit. "She got as far as the lobby. I found the cart tucked into a nook and no Tula. Even though I waited and waited. So I'm bringing the baked goods to Brenda, but where is Tula, Evelyn? What's happened to her?"

"One way to find out," said Evelyn. She called one of the interns to take over the desk and moved toward the coffee kiosk. "Drop off your baked goods and let's go see our old friend, Seamus McCord. If Tula was in the lobby, the camera should show her, right? We know they've got the lobby well covered."

"Great idea."

They dropped the cart with Brenda at the Angel Wing kiosk. She promised to call Food Services and get it picked up once the baked goods had been unloaded. Anne mentioned two missing fritters as she handed Brenda the five dollars, and Brenda laughed.

"Polly Periwinkle," she guessed.

Anne nodded.

"She loves those peach fritters, and I always hold two back when she's working. One for her and one for Ted, but I'm not sure if Ted really gets his or if Polly eats it on the way home, because Ted is thin and wiry and Polly isn't. But no one has a kinder heart," she concluded, then smiled Anne's way. "Except for you, Anne."

"Brenda, how sweet." Her words blessed Anne, but right now all she could think of was Tula. None of this made sense, and for a woman who loved solving TV and paperback mysteries long before their screen and book reveal, Anne was feeling like a dunce about this one. What wasn't adding up?

Everything.

And it only got worse when they got to security and Seamus wasn't there.

"When will he be in?" asked Anne.

"Not until ten," said the plain-clothed woman who answered their knock on the door. Her badge said C. TEMPLE. "He had an appointment this morning."

"But we need to see the lobby footage now," explained Evelyn.

The woman looked incredulous. "No one sees this footage except us and admins."

"We have permission from Garrison."

She looked around, doubtful. "And where exactly is this permission?"

"He sent it down to Seamus McCord. On Monday."

Anne's answer didn't make headway. "Well, it's Friday, ladies. Seamus isn't here, and Mr. Baker is at a Community Medical Council meeting until midafternoon according to his schedule, so there's no way I can allow you to view those tapes."

"Even if a woman's life may be in danger?" Anne put the question to her bluntly.

"Whose life and what makes you think so?"

An idea inspired Anne. "You have an employee file, correct? With pictures?"

"Sure, it's required for name badges and access points."

"You can look at the tapes," Anne told her. "Tula Manchester, she was wheeling a cart of bakery items—"

"I know Tula," said the woman. "Anyone who likes community theater in Charleston knows Tula."

"Go see what happened to her," Evelyn urged. "If we can't look, you can. She was supposed to get to the Angel Wing kiosk and didn't. Now it could be indigestion, but Tula would have called in to Food Services if she had to run home. Or it could be foul play. When all is said and done, I'd like Tula to know we didn't make assumptions when it came to her life."

The woman accepted that. "I'll check. And FYI, I'm Carrie Temple. So you know who you're talking to."

"Thank you, Carrie." She faced Evelyn after Carrie left them to wait for results. "I'm not sure if I want her to see what happened, or I want it to be that nothing happened and Tula just walked away. It's not like she could be kidnapped from the lobby, right?"

Evelyn agreed. "Kidnappings are more intrinsic to dark alleys, I believe. Rarely in a crowded, busy hospital lobby. Although people have walked right out of hospitals carrying stolen babies, so things do happen."

"Fortunately, Tula isn't a baby."

Carrie returned less than five minutes later. "I've watched the tape three times. She enters the lobby and delivers to the lobby coffee kiosk and the café. And then, as she approaches this wing, she pulls out her phone. There's a short conversation. She doesn't appear to be saying much, then she turns and her back is to the camera."

"To all of them?" asked Anne.

"Pretty much. I don't think it was intentional, she simply turned away from the people coming in and out. She shoves the phone in her pocket, pushes the cart into the alcove with the plaque thanking the Gaylord family for its contributions to Mercy Hospital, and leaves through the main entrance."

"Does she stay gone?" wondered Anne. "Or did she come back?"

Carrie pulled out her phone, hit a number, and turned on the speakerphone. "Let's find out." When a woman answered, Carrie asked her if Tula was in the cafeteria.

"No, and I'm worried," said the woman. Anne recognized Shakilah's voice. "Tula is so exacting about everything she does. She'd never just leave me stranded like this. This is totally out of character."

"Could her son be in trouble?" asked Anne. If Tula did have a son, the kitchen manager would likely know about it.

There was a momentary hesitation on the other end. "Son?" Shakilah echoed. "Tula doesn't have any kids."

No son. So who was this young man?

Anne exchanged looks with Evelyn. "My mistake, of course. I saw her with a young man the other day and I assumed—"

"She's helping a friend's son get settled in town," Shakilah said. "But even if he were in trouble, she'd have called me. No, this isn't like her at all. Not our Tula."

Carrie disconnected the call and faced the women. "So something happened, clearly, but it's nothing we can address. She wasn't coerced, wasn't endangered..."

"I don't think we know that," argued Evelyn.

"Not that we saw, in any case." Carrie seemed genuinely sympathetic. "Is there a way for y'all to check it out? How close are you with her?"

"Not close at all," Anne replied. "But you're right, we'll figure out a way to track this down. I know it's out of your purview."

Carrie handed them each a business card from the security office. "Keep me or Seamus informed, all right? If there's something shady going on in the hospital, we don't want to be caught flat-footed."

Anne tucked the card into her pocket. "We will."

Carrie went back into the office.

Anne and Evelyn walked back up the hall. When Evelyn crooked a finger toward the vintage records room, Anne followed. She shut the door tightly behind herself and swung around. "Evelyn, what are we going to do? What's going on? Where did she go?"

Evelyn raised her hands. "I have no idea. If that wasn't her son with her the other night, who was it? Byron's child, perhaps? His son? I can't imagine another explanation, which means Byron went on with his life, right? Anne, are you sure he resembled Byron?" pressed Evelyn. "Or was Byron on your mind and you saw a resemblance because of that?"

"Good grief, I'm not flaky. It was a very handsome young man who looked a lot like Byron did thirty years ago. A touch younger, though. I know what I saw, Ev."

Evelyn sighed. "I'm sure you did. I'm just clutching at straws. My brain is feeling scrambled. It's like there are all these threads going every which way, zigging and zagging, like a spiderweb."

A spiderweb.

Multiple circles, connecting to an inner core.

The image clicked into Anne's brain like a light-bulb moment. "But what does every spider web have in common?" she asked Evelyn.

Evelyn shook her head.

"A spider. The spider forms the center circle and everything spins and weaves out from there, correct?"

"Yes." Evelyn elongated the word as if wondering why they were talking about spiders.

"So," breathed Anne, "if Byron is the spider, everything weaves out from him. A relationship with Tula, a relationship with his cousin, his grandpa, Dr. Schlater, those little boys."

Evelyn looked confused. "But if he's gone, how does he draw all of them together?"

Anne snapped her fingers, wheeled around, and headed for the door. "That's exactly what we need to find out, and I'm going to spend every spare moment I have today plotting this out. The answer is there. Somewhere. We just need to find out where."

Anne swung into the gift store after lunch and bought a spiral notebook and a multicolor pack of pens from Joy. "I should have thought of this before," she explained as she handed over her debit card. "I'm a visual learner. I'm going to draw myself a web and fill in the spaces. And when I'm done, we'll know which way to go."

Joy didn't look convinced, but she did look encouraged. "I think that's a great idea. Can I join you after work?"

Something in her voice made Anne pause. "Are you all right?"

"Yes." Joy busied her hands fixing several beautiful floral arrangements that needed no fixing.

"Then come out to our place," Anne told her. "We're ordering supper in tonight."

"I don't want to be the fifth wheel at a romantic supper while Addie's out of town," Joy protested.

Anne laughed and linked her arm through Joy's. "No such thing, Ralph will either be reading something very inspirational or snoring in his recliner. That's his Friday night norm, and after a busy week, I'm fine with that. You and I can look this over, all right?"

Joy's eyes brightened. "I'd like that, Anne."

"Good." Anne wasn't sure what had dimmed her new friend's gaze that day, but there was nothing like trying to save a life, solve a crime, and find a body, dead or alive, that took one's mind off their troubles.

And it would be good to look at the facts together. It sounded like a perfectly good, quiet evening, right up until Evelyn sent out a group text shortly after two o'clock. ALERT!

Anne's brows shot up at the initial text, but Evelyn did admire a good piece of well-presented drama.

I'VE FOUND TULA MANCHESTER'S REAL ADDRESS AND SHE IS NOT THERE. REPEAT: SHE IS NOT THERE. CAR IS STILL IN PARKING GARAGE HERE. WE NEED TO FIND HER. STAT!

Shifting Winds Home for Erring Women

May 1912

They know.

I'm not sure how. I have been the soul of discretion, as have my patients, but somehow word has gotten out that I've been helping Black mothers at risk.

Normally there is no need of my assistance. Their community has many good women who attend births as I do. But now and again I've been called to stand in, to assess and direct and guide those beautiful babies into the world safely. It has been an honor to do so, but it has been in silence. The hallowed silence of absolute necessity.

Somehow the silence has been broken.

They are coming for me.

I will not stay and let them take me. I've done much good here and have much to be thankful for. My mission in life was to help women and bring health, and I've accomplished that.

I don't dare say goodbye to my precious Miriam or her kind and strong husband, or their three beautiful children, two girls and a boy, a solid, strapping lad whose voice will be heard one day. I know this, as I knew it about Robert, so long ago.

It will be dark soon.

A crowd will gather.

I am putting my journals in a quiet spot in the old schoolhouse where Miriam and Cora and Jacob learned side by side with pregnant young mothers. It served a purpose, as did I. And now it will serve one more.

I will go north. I can help there and not be found, for the cities there teem with people. I will pray for my beloveds here...and help others there.

My time here is done.

Helen Davis Cooper
In the Year of Our Lord 1912
In God and God alone do I trust.

Chapter Seventeen

ANNE ANSWERED QUICKLY. JOY'S HOUSE AFTER SHIFTS. SHIRLEY, I'LL DRIVE YOU HOME AFTER. WHAT HAVE WE GOTTEN OURSELVES INTO?

Three thumbs-up emojis came back to her. The quick show of support said all four women were on the same page.

A flurry of afternoon discharges kept Anne on her toes until three thirty. By the time she signed out, it was nearly four. She texted Ralph as she walked to Joy's. Shirley and Evelyn had already arrived.

They didn't take time for drinks. Not this time.

Anne pulled out her notebook and set it on Joy's kitchen table. "I only had time for a cursory scribble, but here's our web," she announced. She pointed to the center. "Byron." And then she indicated the lines coming off the center and the names affiliated with Byron or his disappearance.

"We're missing a few connections," observed Shirley.

Anne made a face. "I noticed the same thing," she confessed. "I thought that once I put it down on paper, it would be easy, but then I realized that there are things on the outside of the web that seem to matter, and how can that be?"

"You mean like Lorilyn?"

"Yes, there's no place for her here."

"And the man you saw who looks like Byron," added Shirley.

"We have no idea if he fits in or if it's sheer coincidence," observed Evelyn. She studied the web. "You've got people here, but no places. Or organizations. Like the hospital, the trauma surgeons. That sort of thing. If Byron is at the center, those things should form some of the branches, shouldn't they?"

"Of course." Anne began filling in lines. She was moving right along, but then she stopped.

Stared at the paper.

And then she lifted her gaze to the other women. "What if Byron isn't at the center?"

Shirley frowned. So did Joy.

But Evelyn smacked a hand to her forehead as if reading Anne's mind. "The manor!"

"Yes." Anne tore out another sheet of paper. In the center she wrote *Wellington Manor* and drew lines out from there, and when she started filling in the references and cross-references, everything fit. In some way, shape, or manner, all the names and places had a connection to Wellington Manor, even if they didn't have a direct connection to Byron.

She took in a deep breath and checked her watch. "Ladies, who's busy tonight?"

"Mama's having Miss Rosie Lee over for supper, and Miss Rosie Lee is bringing it along, so I'm free," announced Shirley.

"James is having supper with his brothers," said Evelyn.

"And Ralph will understand," Anne added. "I know we were going to the manor tomorrow, but I don't want to wait that long. Not with Tula missing."

"Tula's missing? What?" Shirley put her hands on her hips. "Way to bury the lede, Sweetness!"

"Oh, I'm sorry, we found out this morning and it's just been hectic. She walked out of the lobby and hasn't been seen since."

"That's what my text was referencing," explained Evelyn. "About her car still being in the parking garage."

Shirley frowned. "Did someone pick her up?"

"I think it's something more nefarious than that," said Anne. "Tula's strange behavior, the spat with Dr. Schlater, him threatening her jobs. That man has more at stake here."

"So does Lorilyn," added Joy.

"So let's figure out why." Anne stood. "Let's face the heat and find out what there is about this beautiful old mansion that ties all of this together. Because now that I see it on paper, I'm pretty sure that's the heart of the matter. One way or another."

Shirley rode with Anne, and Joy and Evelyn followed in Evelyn's car. They parked at Old St. Andrew's church like they had before, and now that they knew where they could squeeze through the bushes surrounding the estate, they went there straightaway.

Anne led the way to the window, then turned. "We have four hours of daylight left. Let's split up. Joy and Evelyn, can you two take the house?"

"Yes." Joy was already drawing the unlocked window open.

"And Shirley, you and I will take the grounds."

"I don't do spiders and snakes," Shirley warned Anne, but Anne waved that off.

"Honey, you are Southern born and bred. Spiders and snakes just come along with the territory, so you cannot pull that on me."

Anne and Shirley headed for the back of the house once Evelyn and Joy had disappeared through the window. Anne sent them a test text. DO YOU HAVE RECEPTION THERE?

A smiley face emoji came back to her.

"Okay." She led the way through the mowed gardens. *Garden* was a generous word, but they'd been gardens at one time, and a couple of them still had little signs posted. SWEET BASIL, read one. And another was labeled CUTTING GARDEN. Other signs were obliterated with time, but the thought of these gardens being used and tended was like touching a page of the past.

There were four outbuildings set distant from the brick manor, and a carriage house that sat fairly close. The roof was worn. Obviously, Lorilyn hadn't financed that repair as yet, but when Anne pressed her face against a window, there didn't seem to be any water damage inside.

The broad carriage house offered no clues. The very emptiness of it seemed to mock her efforts.

Shirley led the way down a winding path that forked in two directions. One took them toward the river. The deepening shadows of late afternoon meant mosquitoes, but Shirley reached into her little bag and withdrew a small bottle of bug repellent. "Mama always keeps these on hand," she told Anne as they misted themselves. "At first I thought it was kind of silly, but I've pulled this out of my purse more often down here than I ever did in Atlanta, and that's a fact."

"I'm just glad you have it," Anne said. Shirley tucked the aerosol away and they took the path quickly, and then not so quickly. The winding path narrowed. Anne had toured the cemetery across the road several times, but there was a big difference between a trimmed historic cemetery and what lay before them here.

Thirty years of Chinese wisteria covered what had probably been thick, lush trees at one point. The invasive plant had found unwilling partners in the far reaches of the Wellington estate, and the thick-trunked vines hung low and high as they girdled the branches of the now-dead trees.

Anne touched Shirley's arm. "I don't want to be a crybaby, but this isn't safe, Shirley."

"The dead trees or the killing vines?" Shirley asked, looking back at her with a smile. "We could have taken the other way and checked out those buildings, but we chose this one, and I will see this through. What are the chances of one of these branches falling now?"

"Considering no one has disturbed them for a time, and we're here now and the wind is picking up, I'd say the chances are increasing exponentially."

Shirley grinned. "Well, I'm up for the challenge. Let's go." They were just about to trudge beneath the lowest hanging branches to re-find the path on the other side of the sprawling tree, when a noise came to them.

Shirley's chin came up.

So did Anne's. She moved back up the path a few steps, straining to see, but the vines kept visibility minimal. "Hello? Evelyn? Joy?"

No answer came.

She was just about to rejoin Shirley when a sound came again.

An inhuman sound.

Like something scraping in a gritty, grinding fashion, the kind of noise that made you think of scary stories teenagers love to share.

Anne wasn't a fan of scary stories.

She looked up. The tree branches were being tugged by the wind and the weight of the vines, but the vine fought the movement, so the sound wasn't coming from there.

The noise came again. Metallic. Maybe. Not wood.

"What is that noise?" She whispered the question to Shirley, and when she noticed the goose bumps on Shirley's arms, she knew the sound was chilling Shirley too.

"It sounds like something from one of those stupid movies, right before the girl runs to hide in the worst place ever with no way out," Shirley whispered back.

She was right.

The sound was eerie, and yet it must have been caused by the wind, because they were alone back there.

Weren't they?

The sound came again, no longer and no shorter than it had squealed before, a long, aching sound, as if something were crying.

Or someone.

Now Anne had goose bumps too.

"Do we go in?" Shirley motioned to the thickly wrapped trees. "Or avoid it at all costs?"

Anne breathed deep and pulled back a vine. "We go in. And pray."

Darkness surrounded her, and it took a minute for her eyes to adjust. The scene inside the wrapped trees was a tangle of green. It was hard to imagine life outside the jungle-like atmosphere, because the vines deadened sound. In here there were no car engines going by on Ashley River Road. There were no voices of neighbors or lawn mowers chugging their way across narrow front yards. A spooky kind of quiet enveloped the trees, as if the vine silenced everything in its quest for domination.

Anne knew there was a building close by, but it was invisible from where they were. The other buildings ran close to the far property line, but this corner was out of the way and absolutely invisible from the road or the house, as if the growth had taken over. Only one building appeared on the plat map for this side of the property.

"It's like a stinkin' vine shroud," said Shirley, only this time she spoke in a normal voice, and Anne nearly jumped out of her skin.

Shirley jumped too. "Ow!"

"Shirley. Are you all right?" Anne peered through the darkness to see what happened.

"I'm fine, you unnerved me is all. Why did you jump?"

Anne cringed. "I wasn't expecting you to talk normal."

"Well, they may be monster vines, but they don't scare me." Shirley withdrew her phone from her pocket and turned on the flashlight feature. Anne did the same. The light gave them a better view of their small circle, but it also showed the path along the ground leading to the left, through more vines and trees. Shirley broke through purposely, swinging the lowest vines up for Anne to follow. They continued, one branch at a time, fighting their way through inches of space. Anne was just about to throw her hands up in defeat when she followed Shirley through another pass.

A small area opened up before them, as if it was meant to be. The vines hadn't grown down here.

They'd arched out, over the roofline of this building, and their travels formed a thick canopy over a two-step entrance into the building. And above those two steps stood a door.

The building was completely invisible from outside the vine-clad woods. The years of growth had encased it. It wasn't very big, nor was it small. About twenty by twenty, Anne estimated, and built along the same lines as the house. The roof held no dormer windows, but seemed to arch up, into the vines, and that only allowed them more of a grip.

The sound came again.

Louder this time. Closer. As if it were coming from this building, a building that had been closed for decades, most likely.

Anne didn't wait to discuss their options. They'd fought their way through, and the door was most likely locked in any case, so she sprang up those two steps and turned the handle.

The door pushed open on a loud groan of hinges that had been left unoiled for a long, long time.

Anne prayed for courage. She'd also like a mask because the dust that rose up to greet them was what they'd expected and never found in the main house.

Four tables sat in a two-by-two formation in the room. Beneath the dust and some old, scattered leaves was a dark wood floor. Each table had four chairs, but a row of eight chairs along the nearby wall indicated the tables could accommodate six if needed. And there in the front, beyond a rogue vine that had broken through the roof, was a teaching desk.

"It's a school." Shirley flashed her light around the area. Dusty, dark images gave them an idea of what had gone on here. On one wall were the remnants of maps, the kind a teacher would tug down with a string and then roll back up like one would a window shade. There were several maps inside one another, a clever system of layering that Anne had seen in a museum years ago.

On the teacher's desk were accoutrements of the time. An ink well. Slates. And a canteen hung on a peg behind her desk. A woodstove was tucked into a corner, too close to the wall by modern standards, but there were no fire codes when this building was put together. The builder had the presence of mind to brick the wall and the floor, though, and Anne gave credit for that.

"I expect it was nice in its time," said Shirley. "Is it listed on the property as a school?" she asked Anne. "Because we'd have noticed that, wouldn't we?"

Anne shook her head. "It's simply listed as wood building," she said. "And look, there's our groaning person." She pointed to the side where a branch had broken loose from the tree. On its own, and hung up with vines, the branch was scraping against the metal grating of a window. Not all the time, but just enough to send chills along unsuspecting spines.

"Do you remember what Wellington's will said?" Shirley asked.

Anne frowned.

"About how Byron valued education."

"A family trait?"

"Well, this place looks like it was outfitted for an early twentieth-century museum if it were cleaned up and we didn't have to worry about the roof caving in on us with the weight of the vines."

Anne hadn't given that a thought, she'd been so surprised to find this spot. "You're right. I'm sure this is dreadfully dangerous. Which means we should explore quickly," she added sensibly, because no way was she leaving this building of artifacts without giving it a good once-over.

She moved to the teaching area. Behind the teacher's desk were signs. Some were biblical quotes, including two Proverbs, and one was a bit of wisdom that read simply To THINE OWN SELF BE TRUE.

She was trying to take a photo of that when her foot caught something else. Something metal. She almost fell but grabbed hold of the chalk shelf beneath the long blackboard. The shelf didn't give way, or she would have fallen, and when she righted herself, she flashed her light toward the metal object. "Shirl."

"Yes?"

"Look."

Shirley came her way as Anne bent and picked up the metal plate. "It's the poem, Shirley."

Shirley's eyes went round. "'The kiss of the sun for pardon, the song of the birds for mirth...'"

"'One is nearer God's heart in a garden than anywhere else on Earth.'"

"The verse on the prescription papers."

"With the X that marked a spot."

Shirley made a face. "How can we find that spot?"

Anne held up her phone. "Let's check the pictures I took, my friend."

When Anne found the right image, she raised it up for Shirley to see and then she studied the dark, dusty room around her. "Where would one hide a treasure?" she wondered out loud.

"If it's a traditional heavy treasure, I would guess the floor," mused Shirley.

"Well, there's an inch and a half of dust on the floor—"

"Evelyn would not be happy about that."

Shirley was right. Anne wasn't all that happy either, but they were here, so... "Bring your light this way." They went back and forth along the wall.

Nothing.

The same held true for the other walls, and the floor looked just as solid as a floor could look except for water damage beneath the hanging wisteria vine.

Anne and Shirley made eye contact. Then they looked at the desk. Then each other.

Anne swallowed hard. "My mother always told me not to open drawers or closets in vacant buildings."

"Sage words. So let's go and call it a day," said Shirley, but Anne couldn't do that. Not when they'd come this far.

"I'll look," she said with a bravado she didn't feel. Critters loved to find lodging in old drawers and dressers, didn't they? "But if anything jumps out at me, come to my rescue, all right?"

Shirley picked up what might have been a broom at one time except all the broomcorn had long since been chewed off the end. She raised it high. "I've got your back."

Anne moved to the desk. It wasn't her back she was worried about. It was her front, actually, as she reached forward and pulled open the center drawer.

Sawdust from chewed-up pencils filled the area. Other than that, the drawer was empty. It was a kneehole desk, so she reached for the top side drawer.

Nothing jumped out, and Anne breathed a sigh of relief. Maybe this would be her lucky day. Maybe...

She opened the deeper bottom drawer.

It resisted her attempt. To counter that, she pulled harder, and still the drawer wouldn't open.

Shirley reached around the desk from her side. She pressed something beneath the top and not only did the drawer spring open, it slammed forward, into Anne's knees. "Ouch!" She wasn't sure which knee to grab, and no way was she sitting down on that floor to grab both, but the sting was quite real.

"Anne, I'm sorry." Shirley hurried to her side. "I didn't know that would happen. I only know about these built-in levers because they have them at the history museum in Atlanta. That desk looked just like this one, so I thought I'd give it a try." She looked so sheepish that Anne had to stop rubbing her knees to hug her.

"I'm fine," she told Shirley. "It was more fear of something leaping out at me than a bump on the shins, and—" She let out a low, long whistle. "Shirley, my friend, what have we here?" She trained her light into the drawer, where it seemed a false bottom had been jarred loose to reveal an old metal box, the kind that antique stores loved to find.

Anne reached in and withdrew the box. It wasn't rusted after being tucked in a drawer for who knew how long, but it was locked. A small but sturdy padlock held bottom and top firmly together. "It's heavier than it looks," she told Shirley.

"Are we taking it?" Shirley looked around nervously, as if anyone would purposely be trapped in the tangle of this wisteria jungle.

"Yes. And we won't worry about opening it until we get out of here. It's not big enough for a body," she added cheerfully.

Shirley groaned, then she moved ahead to lead them out of the vine-covered thicket. They'd gotten almost to the edge when something moved to their left.

Shirley turned. Surprise made a perfect O of her mouth but before Anne could turn around to see what surprised her friend, a thick-gloved hand clamped around her face from behind. "Don't make a sound or she's a goner. You hear me?" The hand around Anne's mouth was joined by one across her throat, leaving no doubt she was going to behave. At least long enough to figure a way out of this.

"Tie her up." It wasn't a rope that landed at Shirley's feet. It was a package of zip ties. Shirley stared at Anne as if willing her to say or do something, but Anne was busy trying to keep her neck in one piece.

Shirley removed a tie from the package.

"Grab a handful. You'll need more than one, and if the two of you behave, I'll leave you here for the bugs to bother while I disappear. If you try anything, I have no problem leaving nonliving things behind. Either way, I'll be long gone."

Anne tried to place the voice.

She couldn't. It didn't sound at all familiar.

Shirley withdrew more zip ties. They were the bigger ones. Thicker. Longer. She approached Anne with such a look of sorrow that Anne longed to reassure her, tell her it was all right. She couldn't of course. Breathing was about all she could handle right now, and the smell of this man's thick glove was making her stomach churn. When Shirley put the thick plastic tie around Anne's wrists, she wasn't sure who felt worse. She or her dear friend.

The man gave a quick jerk of his knee to the back of Anne's knees once her hands were tied. The sudden movement took her legs out from under her. She collapsed onto the wood-strewn ground. "Feet now."

Shirley was weighing her options. Anne saw it in her eyes. This man presented a real danger. Possibly mortal danger. But what could they do at this moment?

Pray.

Anne closed her eyes, willing herself to stay calm. Prayer was her go-to answer for everything. Always. Prayer and action often became prayer-in-action.

Did this man know there were others?

He answered the question as she thought it. "And don't be thinking your little friends are going to come rescue you," he snarled, and when Shirley didn't tighten Anne's ankles enough, he took his hand from her mouth and jerked the plastic tie so tight that her eyes watered. Still, she was not about to give this brute the satisfaction of seeing her cry. As if.

"What are you after?" she asked.

He swung around to face her as he yanked off a piece of shiny gray duct tape, and when she realized who it was, her gut went tight. "Who are you? Byron's son?"

He curled his lip. "His nephew, and one of the few Wellingtons who isn't afraid to go after what I want and deserve no matter what the cost. My family got jerked out of the inheritance years ago. I'm just here to right an old wrong. And if you do this my way, no one has to get hurt."

"You were with Tula," said Shirley.

He frowned at her. "Your friend here has a big mouth. If she'd left well enough alone none of this would be necessary. I had it all worked out, but then you started snooping around. Asking questions that didn't need to be asked. But that's over now."

Keep him talking. Anne had seen that on enough mystery and suspense shows, how buying time could give rescuers the narrow window they needed.

Except their rescuers were in a similar boat, if what he said was true. If she could keep him talking, maybe there'd be a chance for some kind of retaliation. "Why are you doing this?"

He looked at her as if she were stupid and then nudged the heavy box. "The treasure. The old reverend's money stash that no one's found for over a hundred years. If we didn't get our fair share of the manor, at least I'll get this." He spat the words out as if doubting her intelligence.

She wasn't stupid, and she'd lifted that box. She wasn't sure what was in it, but it wasn't gold coin. "What do you think is in that box?" she asked.

"Shut up."

He moved toward her, and she used the last few seconds to push his buttons. "It's not money," she told him, and that was enough to make him pause. "Or gold. It feels like books." Those were the last words she got out before he slapped the tape over her mouth.

He glowered at her and turned away. "Your turn." He reached out and yanked Shirley forward. "I see the fight in your eyes, lady, and I'm just going to tell you it's not worth it to risk your life over something that means nothing to you and everything to me."

"Money's never worth it." Shirley looked him straight in the eye. "God's riches are worth a lot more than man's."

"Then be sure to pray for me when I'm gone, and I'll take my share of God's riches too." He rolled his eyes and pulled the zip tie so tight around Shirley's wrists that she winced.

Think, Anne. Think. What can you do to stall him?

And then another thought occurred.

Maybe she didn't want to stall him. Maybe he meant what he said. Maybe he'd walk away with the box and they'd all go on their merry way once they were found.

Or he's already hurt Joy and Evelyn and you're next.

She preferred option one, thank you very much.

She pushed thoughts of death aside, but the thought of being at this man's mercy was a gut punch. And yet, she was out of choices.

The hopelessness of the situation didn't just make her sad.

It made her angry.

But there was little to do to appease that anger with bound hands and feet and mouth. When Shirley was trussed up in similar fashion, the man stood up.

He looked huge from her angle on the ground. He wasn't, but he wasn't small either, and they'd reached the moment of truth. He'd shown no gun, but a gun wouldn't be a good idea in this area. Surely a neighbor would hear.

But that left a wide range of other weapons at this Wellington cousin's disposal.

The Lord is my Shepherd. I shall not want.

The beautiful words of the twenty-third psalm filled Anne's mind. Words inspired by God, given to His people. Sweet words of comfort.

The man studied them, as if weighing options, then he jerked his chin as if dismissing them and reached down for the box. He pulled it up and gave it a little shake.

No coin rattled inside.

Anne lifted her brows.

"Paper money spends just as good as gold." He snarled the words but sounded the tiniest bit worried. He shook it back and forth twice, and each time his expression drew down deeper.

He stared at the box, then Anne. His gaze narrowed. "You think you're so smart?"

She looked at him.

Right at him.

And nodded.

No matter what else happened today, she was smart, she was capable, and no two-bit thief looking for an easy out was going to take that away from her, although it was potentially a somewhat stupid sword to fall on, considering her current situation.

He turned to go, then paused. Glanced around. And for just a moment he seemed to realize the situation he was leaving them in. The dense thicket. Bound and gagged. The heat and humidity and air thick with bugs. He hesitated, then reached into his back pocket.

Anne closed her eyes and prayed.

So did Shirley. Anne knew this because she knew Shirley. *Where two or three are gathered together in My name...*

Those sweet words would sustain her.

She didn't open her eyes. She didn't want to see him pull out a weapon. She kept her eyes on God, on Jesus, her Savior. When she heard a soft thud, her eyes shot open.

A box cutter. About twelve feet in front of them.

Her gaze shot to his and for a moment he didn't look quite so awful and angry. "By the time you get over to that and figure out a way to use it without slitting your wrists, I'll be long gone. But at least you won't die in here." He ducked away then, pushing through the heavy, gnarled vine-covered branches on his own, with the heavy box weighing down each step.

Anne started to wriggle toward the box cutter.

A sharp branch caught her hip and tumbled her over.

Shirley lay back and began to roll toward the blade. The low branches, vines, and ground litter made it hard, but bless her, she kept at it, doing a log roll over awful ground in an attempt to get that knife. The eerie silence of the vine-clad grove seemed surreal now, but all Anne could think of was getting free, getting out of here, and finding Evelyn and Joy.

And then explaining all of this to Ralph, who wasn't going to be any too happy about it. But he'd be less happy if she didn't live through it, so she scooched her way to a tree trunk, tried not to think about what was living on this forested floor, and pushed herself back up into a sitting position just as Shirley got close to the blade.

It wasn't easy, but at least he'd tied their hands in front of them. Behind would have made things so much harder.

Shirley had finally gotten to the knife. She hunched up and forward, not an easy task when one is bound and gagged, but when she was able to grasp the box cutter with her fingers, she raised it up, triumphant. She started toward Anne. It was slow progress, but she was making it happen, inch by inch, the box cutter gripped in one hand.

Anne met her halfway. She held out her wrists.

Shirley winced, but then her nursing skills kicked in. Clutched between the fingers of her right hand, and with little space to maneuver, she sawed through Anne's wrist ties. The first thing Anne did when her hands were free was to yank that stupid duct tape off her face.

Ouch!

She pulled off Shirley's too, then made short work of freeing her friend's wrists and ankles and her own ankles too.

When they were free, Anne reached out and hugged Shirley, but not for long. "We've got to go quietly, in case he's not gone, but we've got to get to Evelyn and Joy."

"We sure do, but I wouldn't mind meeting up with him along the way when surprise is on my side." Shirley whispered the words, but her blunt tone underscored her feelings. "I'd teach him a lesson or two, let me tell you."

They crept forward.

It felt funny, without the box. Not because Anne needed treasure, but because the box was part of the mystery. Part of the whole web.

What was in it? And why was it left locked away in the cabin?

As they drew closer to the tangle's edge, where the sidewalk shone more brightly in the late-day sun, a series of noises startled them. Anne grabbed her friend's arm. "Get down." They crouched again, the dangling leaves touching Anne's face and arms, making her itch with the sensation.

Her heart raced.

Shirley looked no better.

Had they worked their way free only to meet up with their captor again? Should they try to flee back into the thick wisteria jungle, or dash into the open?

"I am not going back there," Shirley whispered, arms folded. Anne knew that when Shirley folded her arms, she meant business. "I'll face whatever is before us in the sunshine, but I'm not willing to die in the darkness. And that's that."

The noise grew closer.

Footsteps. Footsteps and voices, and when Anne and Shirley bent low to see what was happening on the sunlit side of the path, three familiar faces looked back at them in relief.

Tula. Cabbie Joe. And Dr. Byron Wellington, who was not one bit dead. Anne had never been happier to see anyone in her life.

Chapter Eighteen

"ANNE!" RALPH'S VOICE RANG OUT above the others less than an hour later. "Anne, are you all right?"

His arms closed around her, and at that moment, she was absolutely, positively all right.

"What happened? What's going on? And why are you scraped up?"

"I blame wisteria and him." Anne hooked a thumb to a nearby police car that was just about to take Frank Connors to prison. "Come on in the house. It's a long story, but first I want you to meet Byron Wellington in person. Because when you do, Ralph, you'll know just why this whole thing was so very important."

As they walked toward the manor Anne saw Byron talking to an officer who was holding the locked box. After a moment both men made their way to the manor's front door, arriving just before Anne and Ralph.

They all gathered in the living room. Byron, Tula, Joe Brown, Evelyn and James, Joy, Shirley, Regina, Anne and Ralph. Ralph had picked up Shirley's mother on the way over, and that spunky woman walked right up to Byron Wellington and gave him the biggest hug and welcome home anyone could imagine, and it made tears well in Anne's eyes to see it.

"I don't know where we should start," Anne said a few minutes later.

"The beginning," Tula said. She looked at Byron. His expression of warmth and empathy put Anne at ease, and when he reached out and took Tula's hand, the action soothed her heart even more.

"I walked away," Byron said simply. "I realized during my internship and residency that God had gifted me as a surgeon. But after seeing so much destruction in the world and then the Bronx, I felt deflated. When the offer from Mercy Hospital came, and my family was urging me to come back home, I took it. A wonderful hospital, a great city, family. Friends." He sent Joe a slight smile. "There was this part of me that felt like the prodigal was coming home and ready to help his hometown. But it wasn't what I expected."

"Jealousy and envy and power struggles?" said Anne.

He nodded. "I wasn't here to get anyone's job. I was here to help. So when the team turned against me, I was hurt."

Tenderhearted.

Abe Jackson had mentioned that specifically, how his esteemed cousin had inherited the Wellington tender heart.

"All I ever wanted to do was to help people, and I did, but when everything blew up over the loss of those boys, I couldn't take it. I wasn't able to cope with the accusations, so I walked away." He grimaced with the admission. "I don't like admitting that. I've forgiven myself for it, but it still seems like a moment of weakness. And yet I couldn't see my way clear to fight my way out of it. So I left Tula and my job and my home and family right after Grandpa died. I never read the will. I put it into the box Grandfather had given me long before, and then I gave the box to Tula…"

"I didn't want to keep it at my house," said Tula. "I couldn't throw it away, so I shoved the whole thing into the least-used corner of the hospital, the dusty old records room. I knew it would never be found—no one's ever cared about what's in there. And then I walked through the lobby that morning—"

"Was that really just ten days ago?" asked Anne of no one in particular. "Because it seems a lot longer."

"It was," Tula told her. "To make matters worse, Dr. Schlater saw what I did later when I grabbed your bag. He'd been threatening my job at the hospital and also at the Ghost Tour for years over a bad check offense that happened when I was going through a hard time. He knew about it and threatened to turn me in to Human Resources. I was so tired of his meanness, but I need my jobs. And when I saw Anne later that day, with the box, I freaked out a little and used an old theater trick of throwing my voice to distract her so I could snatch the bag from her. I'm sorry." She directed this at Anne. "When I realized you'd found the will and were asking about Byron, all I could see was his life being messed up again and Dr. Schlater outing me because of his involvement in the scandal. He saw me in the hallway years ago when the private detective hired by Abe Jackson skewered Schlater with Dr. Morthauser's confession."

That was the incident Abe had told them about, how his detective had gotten a guilt-ridden surgeon to open up about Schlater's intentional attack.

"Now, thirty years later, I'm afraid Schlater still won't want his reputation ruined, even though he thinks nothing of wrecking someone else's life."

"So you took the bag."

Tula nodded. "I first heard from Frank Connors a few weeks ago. He knew enough Wellington family history to fool me into thinking he wanted to clean up Byron's legacy. Even so, I wouldn't admit I knew where Byron was, because it wasn't my secret to tell. I was absolutely gullible, maybe because he reminded me of Byron or maybe because I wanted things cleaned up at long last. But Frank didn't care about Byron. What he was really after was treasure and finding some stupid treasure map, but when we looked in that box, there was nothing like that. He figured you must have taken it," she told Anne.

"I wonder if he was watching us and waiting for us to come here," Anne said.

"I think he must have been," said Tula. "Anyway, that's when I began to realize that he wasn't really here to help but to take what didn't belong to him. When I heard that someone had messed with Joy's house, I started to wonder if Frank had done it. I was in the café when you were talking with the preservation lady," she added. "My back was to you, but I heard all your talk about Wellington Manor. I shared it with Frank. He would have been the only person besides me who knew what you were talking about at the café. I'm sorry, Joy." Her apology rang with sincerity. "I never meant for anything bad to happen. Just the opposite, in fact."

"I stayed in touch with Tula," said Byron. He squeezed Tula's hand lightly. "I didn't want to lose such a treasured friendship. Or love," he added softly. "She was caring for her sick mother when I left, and I felt like my stress only added to her issues. I wasn't the same person anymore, and a part of me felt that I didn't deserve her or her love or a full life. I was a lost soul, and I floundered. She couldn't leave, and I couldn't stay. I contacted her once I got resettled and we've stayed in touch, but when she called me this morning, I realized things had gotten out of control."

"I told him that Frank was scaring me. And that's all he had to hear," she finished, smiling up at him.

The front door opened, and Abe Jackson came through the door.

The minute he and Byron laid eyes on one another, Byron shot up, off the chair, and crossed the room to greet him.

They hugged, clapping one another on the back. And then they hugged some more.

Anne couldn't hear what was said, but it didn't matter. Abe had told them exactly what he'd do if he ever got the chance to see Byron again, and Anne was pretty sure that's exactly what happened.

When Abe joined them in the grand and spacious living room, he swept the room a curious look. "Does anyone else notice that this isn't the dusty, abandoned house we all expected it to be? Joe, do you dust?"

Joe Brown sent him a look of mock horror. "Not if I can help it." "Then who?"

A policeman came to the door leading into the expansive dining room with the missing rug and pictures. At his side stood Lorilyn Cochran. She took one look at the gathering, specifically at Byron, and seemed shattered. But then she spoke softly to the policeman, waited for his nod, and entered the room. When she got into the center of the circled group she said, "Hello, Byron. My name is Lorilyn Cochran. I'm your cousin."

Byron, Joe, and Abe exchanged looks of surprise.

"My great-great-grandmother was Helen Davis."

"The midwife." Evelyn's brows lifted. "The midwife who came here to run the home for unwed mothers and did so with unprecedented success."

"My great-grandmother Miriam was Reverend Wellington's child," explained Lorilyn. "Neither one acknowledged it, and Helen pretended to be a widow all her days. Because of her amazing work here, no one ever challenged her, but later generations knew. I have the DNA report here if you need to see it." She set it on the table. "I'm not after anything. Not money or the house—"

"Well." Anne tilted her head. "You do love this place, Lorilyn. You've made that quite clear."

"Of course I do, and I was so angry with you"—she faced Byron—"for abandoning it. I've kept it up as best I could, but we're not rich. I had two daughters to raise, so I'd occasionally sell items I found here to pay for upkeep."

"The rug. And the paintings." Evelyn motioned toward the dining room.

"Yes," Lorilyn acknowledged. "And a few other things. It made sense to sell off some to save the whole, but I had no permission to do that, and I apologize. Sincerely. I just couldn't see the house my great-great-grandmother sacrificed so much for fall apart from neglect, not when there's so much history here. I've hunted for that history from day one, and have never found it, but I think you have." She pointed to the heavy metal box. "This may help." She raised a small metal key. "My great-grandmother kept this key in her silverware chest, then Mama did the same until it was my turn. And now I think we have the lock it fits. May I?"

The box.

Anne wanted to fist-pump the air and shout "yes!" but it wasn't her box or her family. Still she was thrilled when Byron looked to the policeman standing by the door, who nodded.

"Please do." It was Byron who spoke. Lorilyn took a breath, crossed the short span to the box, knelt beside it, and plied the key. It fit.

It unlocked the box without so much as a whimper of metal on metal.

She removed the key and set it aside. And then she raised the lid.

Notebooks filled the box to capacity.

Turn-of-the-century writing journals, book upon book, and when Lorilyn lifted the top one, tears streamed down her face. "My mother knew these existed. We just didn't know where. Helen never told Miriam, but before she passed she told her granddaughter—my grandmother—the truth about everything. Times being what they were, Grandma wasn't willing to sully the family name or Helen's memory with the truth of Miriam's illegitimate birth. But then one day she told my mother. Then, when my mother told me, she mentioned remembering her grandmother telling her that Helen had kept journals of her years as a midwife. I realized Helen's journals could be someplace on the estate."

Evelyn snatched a clutch of tissues from her purse and handed them over quickly.

"Thank you." Lorilyn wiped her eyes and blew her nose. She dragged one finger across the top of the first book and sighed. "Helen Davis wasn't just a midwife. She was everything a friend or mother or sister or neighbor could want. The gardens around the house were all started by her. She raised food for an army and shared it. She made clothing for mothers and babies and neighbors. She was truly a Proverbs 31 woman, the kind who rarely tired, who welcomed any and all, and in a time when it was against the law for her to treat anyone but white women, she cared for anyone who called on her, regardless the color of their skin." Lorilyn sighed. She clutched the journal as if holding something special. So special. "She fell in love with our great-grandfather while he was studying for the ministry, and when she realized she was pregnant, she moved on because an out-of-wedlock baby would have ruined his calling, and she saw what a gift he had. So she stepped away in an act of sacrificial love."

"What brought her back?" asked Shirley. "He was a pastor of a successful church then. What brought her to Charleston?"

"He went to see her after his wife died. She was a skilled midwife and he wanted to turn the manor into a home for women in trouble. When he realized that Helen had borne him a child, he brought them here to have his love and protection all of their days. It made Shifting Winds a twofold mission for him."

"They never married." Evelyn looked a little miffed by that until Lorilyn continued.

"They pledged a vow of friendship and celibacy, making Shifting Winds and their children their first love. The care and treatment of women in need. Helen did it out of love for midwifery and Robert out of compassion and regret that Helen had spent those years alone to protect his reputation."

"That's an amazing story," breathed Joy. "I think I need one of those tissues myself, Evelyn."

Lorilyn wiped her eyes again. "It was never about acknowledgment or praise for Helen. It was always about a life of service and joy. She planted the gardens, harvested them, helped the cook put up food for the winter, and shared the bounty with others. When it was time for Miriam to go to high school, Robert and Helen feared how the other students might treat her. So Robert had the back building restored as a schoolhouse. They hired a teacher at first, but later on Helen took over some of the teaching. I expect that's why the journals were found there."

In this new context that made perfect sense.

Anne folded her tissue in her fist. "What happened when Robert died?"

"It's said that the townspeople discovered Helen was helping women of color. They formed a mob, and they were going to come for her. Who knows what they would have done?" Sorrow deepened the tiny furrow between her eyes. "They were set to burn the manor but when they got here, she was gone. She'd moved on."

Helen Davis's sacrifices and service had been taken for granted over the years. But now these journals could bring her story back into the light, and tell of her courage as well as the courage of the women she cared for.

Regina yawned, and Anne took that as a signal. She stood. So did the others. The Wellington crew needed time to talk on their own. And Anne and the other ladies needed time to clean up and rest.

Ralph raised a hand when they got to the church parking lot several minutes later. "I'd like everyone to come over to our place for barbecue on Sunday," he announced. "I'm marinating ribs in cherry juice."

One of Anne's favorites.

"And I can put a brisket in the smoker tomorrow," offered James. "With just the two of us, cooking a full-on brisket is way too much, and cooking a small one just doesn't do the same thing."

"When you're right, you're right," Ralph agreed. "Two o'clock?"

"Two is perfect."

"You know we pick up Addie at noon," Anne reminded him when they got into the car.

"And she'll have a whole lot of folks who will want to hear her horse stories," said Ralph with a grin. "And barbecue. And that, my dear, will be a good day."

Chapter Nineteen

"THAT WAS MELT-IN-YOUR-MOUTH BRISKET, JAMES." Anne smiled his way as folks filled their plates with desserts. "I've never had better."

James grinned. He had a splash of Southern aristocracy about him, but he did like to cook for a crowd.

"So what's going on with Byron and Tula?" asked Shirley. "Any update there?"

"Tula is going to North Carolina to visit him," said Anne. "They aren't jumping into anything, but I told him at our age, it's better to jump into things, because who knows when the good Lord will call us home? He laughed…but I think I convinced him."

"And the manor?"

"Byron is giving the house to the preservation society, the journals to Lorilyn, and the contents of the house are being sold at an exclusive antique auction. The proceeds are to be divided between the heirs that, in his words, got the shaft."

"Oh, that's so nice of him."

Anne nodded. "It sure is."

"Where will Cabbie Joe live?" asked Evelyn. "He's had a rough time according to what you gals said."

"Abe is taking Joe's advice about a foundation to help folks who are teetering on the brink, and Joe's going to head it up. They haven't come up with a name for it yet, but it'll probably have something to do with bridges. Joe feels like lots of folks fall apart when that first bridge gets washed out underneath them, and he'd like them to have solid footing to land on. And Abe is having Joe move into the caretaker's house on the island. Abe's caretaker was ready to retire but didn't want to leave him in a lurch, and Joe needed a home, so it worked out well. Joe will have to dust, but he said he was willing to learn."

"That's great," Shirley said after swallowing a bite of cake. "So all's well that ends well, and what a couple of weeks we've had. I can't remember the last time I had this much excitement in such a short time."

"I was going to say the same thing," said Evelyn, "but I see a girl with a very determined look on her face coming this way with books about horses. Anne, I believe there are some serious equestrian studies in your future."

Anne laughed as Addie skipped onto the patio with pictures of camp and the illustrated books. Anne hugged her precious granddaughter and winked at Shirley. "As you and I found out, we are never too old to learn a few new tricks, Shirley. Although I will never look at wisteria fondly again. And that's a fact."

Shirley gave her a round-eyed look and laughed. "Me neither, my friend. Me neither."

Dear Readers!

Oh, how things have changed! Helen Davis's life in Charleston was brazen for the times although somewhat protected by the auspices of the church's approval and God's holy teachings. But even then, she skated a thin line of respectability, didn't she? And what a love story, star-crossed lovers whose pledge of mission and vision kept them apart but the home for unwed mothers together.

We live in very different times now, but we recognize that there are still problems among people. Problems that could be solved with the love and faith that Helen Davis and Robert Wellington didn't just show—they lived.

I had such a great time writing this story. The amazing and wonderful Susan Downs, one of my great Guideposts editors, gave me the idea for the Home for Erring Women and it was perfect. I hope you enjoyed reading it as much as I enjoyed writing it! And you know I love to hear from readers, so email me at loganherne@gmail. com or friend me on Facebook and visit my website ruthloganherne. com. I'd love to get to know you!

And welcome to the Miracles and Mysteries of Mercy Hospital!

With love,

Ruthy

A shout-out to the poem used in the story, "God's Garden" by Dorothy Frances Gurney. We see the verse that's highlighted in the book on signs and wall hangings and inspirational items, but the whole poem is rarely seen, and Dorothy's name is often left off. So here's the poem with the author credited... So beautiful!

God's Garden

The Lord God planted a garden
In the first white days of the world,
And He set there an angel warden
In a garment of light enfurled.
So near to the peace of Heaven,
That the hawk might nest with the wren,
For there in the cool of the even
God walked with the first of men.
And I dream that these garden-closes
With their shade and their sun-flecked sod
And their lilies and bowers of roses,
Were laid by the hand of God.
The kiss of the sun for pardon,
The song of the birds for mirth,
One is nearer God's heart in a garden
Than anywhere else on earth.
For He broke it for us in a garden
Under the olive-trees
Where the angel of strength was the warden
And the soul of the world found ease.
Dorothy Frances Gurney

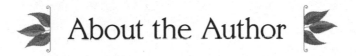

About the Author

WITH OVER SIXTY PUBLISHED NOVELS and novellas to her credit, *USA Today* bestselling author Ruth Logan Herne is absolutely living her dream of being a published author, a task that she's pretty sure the Holy Spirit promised her a long time ago. She and her husband, Dave, own a very popular pumpkin farm in Western New York, and during the busy fall season she takes some time from writing sweet books to bake amazingly delicious things for the farm customers. A mother and grandmother, Ruthy loves God, her family, her beautiful country, dogs, cats, mini donkeys, and growing things. She can often be seen with coffee, Diet Mountain Dew, and chocolate and sees no irony in the mix. Not one she'll admit to, anyway. ☺

Friend her on Facebook, visit her website ruthloganherne.com, and feel free to email Ruthy at loganherne@gmail.com. She'd love to hear from you!

An Armchair Tour of Charleston

THE ANGEL OAK TREE ON JOHNS ISLAND

I think that I shall never see
A poem lovely as a tree...
—Joyce Kilmer

I love nature. I love growing things, teasing them to life, and then selling what I grow. I live on a farm in Western New York. Up here, in the Northeast Woodlands, if you don't mow it, a forest grows. It's the nature of the land! And, being part dryad, I love trees. I love shade, I love leaves, I love how we visualize the change of seasons through trees. North Country changes are definitive because our seasons are distinct.

It's different in the South, but one thing is the same: the appreciation of trees. When I saw pictures of the Angel Oak, it was instant love. The sprawling limbs, drooping branches, moss, gnarls and burls and thickness of a long-lived tree are witness to so much history. Can you imagine a talking tree? What five hundred years of watching could reveal?

Looking like something out of a Tolkien novel or a Harry Potter scene, the Angel Oak Tree attracts local visitors and tourists. Located at 3688 Angel Oak Road, the Johns Island tree offers quiet testimony to the past and hope for the future.

The tree is thought to be one of the oldest live oak trees east of the Mississippi River. It is 65 feet tall and 28 feet around, and an area of 17,000 square feet is shaded by a "crown" that stretches out like thick-limbed tentacles. The largest branch is 187 feet long.

This Southern beauty has survived hurricanes, floods, and earthquakes. It was damaged by Hurricane Hugo in 1989. It recovered from that onslaught and continues to grow.

Live oaks generally grow more outward than upward. Because it is centuries old, the Angel Oak has done both. It branches out in every direction. Some branches hit the ground, dive beneath, and pop back up, new growth from an aged tree. The tree doesn't house angels, although there is plenty of room for them. The estate was originally owned by Justus and Martha Angel. Hence the name...

The tree is now property of the City of Charleston and development anywhere near the tree is taken very seriously because the Angel Oak isn't just a tree in Charleston. It's a living segment of Charleston history.

Good for What Ails You

REGINA'S LEMON ICEBOX CAKE

Icebox cake is a wonderful way to have your cake and eat it too in the heat of summer. This recipe takes an old Victorian shortbread cookie with bits of rosemary (often called the "love" cookie!) to offset the delightfully lemon taste of the pudding. You can add 1 teaspoon lemon extract to the cookie dough, but Regina finds that too much lemon can overpower the subtle accent of the rosemary…and we never argue with Regina! You can use canned lemon pie filling or lemon curd…. And you can use packaged shortbread cookies. But Regina is old-school Southern and she likes things done right and that means right there in her Charleston kitchen!

Victorian Shortbread Cookies
Ingredients:

1½ cups butter   2¾ cups flour

⅔ cup sugar   ¼ teaspoon salt

2 tablespoons chopped fresh rosemary

Directions:
Cream butter and sugar. Mix in flour, rosemary, and salt until thoroughly blended. Chill for about an hour.

Roll out to ¼-inch thickness and cut into either round or rectangular shapes. Prick with fork lightly to avoid over-puffing. Line cookie sheet with parchment paper and bake at 375 degrees just until sides hint golden. Remove cookies from parchment and let cool completely.

Lemon Pie Filling
Ingredients:

1 cup white sugar	1½ cups water
2 tablespoons flour	4 egg yolks
3 tablespoons cornstarch	½ cup lemon juice
¼ teaspoon salt	2 tablespoons butter

Directions:
Mix sugar, flour, salt, and cornstarch. Add water. Heat over medium heat, stirring constantly until mixture comes to a boil. Whisk egg yolks in separate bowl. Drizzle some of hot mixture into egg yolks to equalize temperature, stirring briskly. Then add this mix back into saucepan. Heat to boiling, stirring. Add lemon juice and butter. Remove from heat. Stir completely, chill thoroughly.

Whipped Cream
Ingredients:
1½ cups heavy cream
½ cup sugar

Directions:
Mix cream and sugar. Whip on high speed until peaks form.

So here's the fun part. Layering the icebox cake.

Line 8" pan with parchment paper.

Layer shortbread cookies over paper.

Spread layer of whipped cream.

Spread layer of lemon filling.

Repeat until pan is full. Top with whipped cream. Garnish with cookie crumbs or lemon zest or fresh blueberries.

Chill overnight or throughout the day.

Serve and enjoy!

Read on for a sneak peek of another exciting book in the Miracles & Mysteries of Mercy Hospital series!

Angels Watching Over Me

by GABRIELLE MEYER

A CRASH OF THUNDER BROUGHT Evelyn Perry's head up from her work. Outside the window of the records department at Mercy Hospital, the wind picked up and a flash of lightning split through the sky. The storm had come out of nowhere.

"Did you know we were supposed to get a storm today?" Evelyn asked her assistant, Stacia Westbrook, who also looked toward the large floor-to-ceiling window in surprise.

"I had no idea," Stacia answered.

The thunder boomed again, rattling the old glass pane. This section of Mercy Hospital was the only one to withstand the great Charleston fire of 1861. Over 575 buildings in the city had been destroyed on that dreadful December night, and many people had feared that the hospital would also fall victim to the flames. But this wing had miraculously survived, along with the statue of an angel that legend said guarded the main entrance. Evelyn was so thankful the wing had survived, along with many of the original documents that were still safely stored in the Vault, a small, windowless room behind the modernized records department.

"I hope it stops before five o'clock," Stacia said. "Emmett and I have plans to go on a picnic to celebrate our one-month anniversary."

Evelyn smiled to herself. Stacia was young, just barely out of college, and had started working in the records department after her graduation in May. In the three months Evelyn had known her, Stacia had dated four different boyfriends, most lasting for less than two weeks. She was notoriously picky, often going on and on about her dates, dissecting them like she would a biology assignment. She was also as cute as a button, and her blond hair and sparkling blue eyes seemed to draw the attention of young men with little effort. If she didn't like one boyfriend, she'd toss him aside for the next. For her to celebrate a one-month anniversary was a big deal.

"Emmett must be a pretty special young man," Evelyn mused as she turned her attention away from the storm and back to her work.

Stacia sighed and put her chin in her hand, her eyes taking on a dreamy, faraway look. "He might be 'the one.'"

"Wow." Evelyn raised her eyebrows, enjoying the dating escapades of Stacia, while thanking God that she had been happily married for almost thirty-five years. "I don't miss dating, even a little."

The sky continued to darken outside as the rain picked up its intensity. Evelyn loved a good storm, but she lived less than a mile west of the hospital, which meant she walked to work. If the storm didn't let up within the next two hours, she'd have to call her husband, James, to come and pick her up. And since he was busy on a secret project today, the last thing she wanted to do was disturb him.

"I can't imagine being married to the same man for thirty-five years, even if he is 'the one.'" Stacia scrunched up her nose. "Isn't it boring?"

A smile warmed Evelyn's lips as she thought back to the journey she and James had shared since the day they said "I do." "It is anything but boring," she told the much younger woman, wishing she had the words to describe all the intricacies of marriage. "James never ceases to amaze me, and thirty-five years later I'm still learning fascinating things about his personality."

"Hmm." Stacia turned back to her desk, truly seeming to puzzle over Evelyn's comment. "I guess I'll have to take your word for it."

Evelyn's desk phone rang, and the little red light started to blink. She pushed aside thoughts of the storm and of Stacia's marital misgivings and answered the phone. "Records Department, how may I help you?"

"Evelyn?" Shirley Bashore's unmistakable voice came through the line.

"Hi, Shirley. What can I do for you?"

"We have a patient who's being transferred from the emergency room to the intensive care unit," Shirley said. "Can you come over to the ER and gather her personal belongings?"

"Of course. I'll be there in a couple of minutes."

"Thank you." Shirley hung up, and Evelyn could only imagine how busy her friend was in the ER. Shirley was one of the most dedicated nurses at Mercy. She had recently moved to Charleston from

Atlanta to take care of her aging mother, and she and Evelyn had become fast friends.

"I have to run over to the ER," Evelyn said to Stacia as she logged off her computer. She never left her program running. The patient files they worked with on a daily basis were confidential and protected by HIPAA, so she was always overly cautious to log out of any computer she accessed in the hospital. "I should be back soon."

Stacia lifted her hand to wave at Evelyn, indicating she heard her.

The records department was on the main floor of the hospital, connected to the modern grand front entrance, not too far away from the gift shop. Though the original part of the hospital had been built in 1829, it had been lovingly maintained and restored over the years and was, by far, Evelyn's favorite part of the hospital. In her opinion, nothing could ever compare to the historical architecture and charm of a nineteenth-century building. But over time, as the hospital had been enlarged, the architects had done a seamless job matching the newer additions to the old. The birthing center and cancer wings were modern and amazing in their own right.

She pushed open the door leading out of the records department and stepped into the main hall. An older couple walked past with a bouquet of mixed flowers and a pink balloon that said WELCOME BABY GIRL. It made Evelyn smile to see their happy faces. Two doctors in white coats were close behind, their heads bent in conversation, and a well-dressed sales rep passed them by heading in the opposite direction, her wheeled bag zipping along the floor on her way out.

Evelyn loved the hustle and bustle of the hospital. She loved the excitement, the energy, and the new challenges each day presented.

Her heels clicked on the hard tile as she walked the short distance to the ER, past a bank of elevators and a grand staircase leading to the second floor. Soft piano music from the main entrance floated gently on the air.

As always, the ER was bursting with activity. The glass doors opened automatically, and Evelyn stepped into the waiting room. She was well known to the staff and waved at the registration gals as she walked past them and into the hub of the department. Shirley stood near the circulation desk, speaking to one of the unit coordinators. She wore her blue scrubs and had a stethoscope around her neck. When she saw Evelyn approach, she turned her full attention to her with a smile.

"Thanks for coming so quickly." Shirley reached behind the desk and lifted a white plastic bag. In the middle of the bag were the words PERSONAL BELONGINGS printed in blue. Underneath were two lines, one for the patient's name and one for the patient's room number. "I'm a little anxious to get these things to a secure location."

Strands of silver weaved through Shirley's black hair, which she pulled back in a simple ponytail. The only hint of adornment she chose to wear was a simple gold cross necklace.

"Why are you so anxious to get these things secured?" Evelyn asked, curious about the items in the bag. It wasn't unusual for Shirley to call the records department to come and collect personal belongings from patients. Often, a person came in alone, especially after an accident, and it took time to contact next of kin. Cell phones, jewelry, wallets, and other valuable items needed to be put somewhere safe until the patient or the patient's family member could collect them. The hospital safe was located in the records department and was as tight and secure as Fort Knox.

Shirley dipped her hand into the bag and pulled out a small object. "The patient we just moved up to the ICU had this in her pocket when she came in." She opened her hand to reveal a beautiful ruby and diamond ring. "It looks really valuable."

Evelyn took the ring out of Shirley's hand and looked at it a little closer. It was an exquisite piece of jewelry, large enough for a man's hand. "I've never seen anything quite like it."

"I didn't have time to look at it closely," Shirley said as she handed Evelyn the bag. "But it needs to be put into the safe as soon as possible. I'm sure Ms. Robertson would be anxious to see it secured as well."

The ER was no place to inspect such a valuable piece of jewelry, so Evelyn slipped it back into the bag. "Can I get the patient's name and room number?"

"Her name is Jeanne Robertson, and she's in ICU room 4120. The police have taken all of her personal information and are trying to locate her family." Shirley shook her head. "But right now she's all alone. She was in a pretty rough car accident and sustained some serious head and leg injuries."

Evelyn winced. "Was anyone else involved?"

"As far as I know, there was only one other person, and he's just being discharged, but the police are waiting to question him." Shirley nodded toward a man walking out of one of the examination rooms. He was dressed in a brown uniform with a postal service badge affixed to the arm. "He was driving a delivery truck and had to swerve to miss a vehicle that had stopped to turn. When he swerved, it pushed Ms. Robertson off the road and she ran right into a tree. Unfortunately, she wasn't wearing a seat belt."

"Oh my," Evelyn said. "He must feel awful."

If the man's troubled face and rounded shoulders were any indication, he *did* feel awful.

"I hate to run," Shirley said, "but we're short-staffed today and I'm needed."

Evelyn smiled and put her hand on Shirley's arm. "No worries. I'll take Ms. Robertson's things back to the records department and get them put away until she's ready for them."

"Thanks, Evelyn." Shirley grabbed a clipboard off the circulation desk and headed toward a patient room.

The bag was heavy as Evelyn walked back toward the sliding glass doors. She passed the delivery man, who glanced at her. His gaze slipped to the bag with Jeanne's name on it and then to Evelyn again. He opened his mouth like he was going to speak, but a police officer approached and captured his attention.

All the way back to the records department, Evelyn could only think of two things: she needed to get the ring secured as soon as possible, and she prayed Ms. Robertson would recover to reclaim her things.

The rain continued to pour outside the hospital as Evelyn reentered the records department. Stacia was on the phone, answering questions about how a person could get their records released to another hospital. Two other staff members were also at work, Pam and Richard. Pam was speaking to a patient at the front desk who was asking for a copy of her daughter's immunization record, while Richard was inputting data into a computer. As the manager of the department, Evelyn oversaw a staff of five individuals. Three of them, Stacia, Pam, and Richard, were full time, and the other two were part time.

Evelyn took the white patient bag into the Vault. It was the original records room, built in 1829, and was full of dozens of file cabinets. The redbrick walls and maple floors were a throwback, but it was the original light fixtures that made Evelyn feel like she was walking into a different era.

She had spent several weeks at the beginning of the summer organizing the room, after years of putting off the task. The disorderly, dusty files had been in need of some attention for as long as she could remember, but there had always been some other project to be completed. Now everything was clean and organized, thanks to the help of a couple of student interns from the College of Charleston. It made Evelyn feel a little bit lighter to know the daunting task was finished. And now, if someone needed a historic file, it would be so much easier to locate. In Evelyn's mind, the old records were just as important and relevant as the newer ones being recorded in the front office.

The hospital safe was also located in this room. It was a huge, walk-in safe, with a heavy, black metal door. Only a handful of hospital staff members had access to the safe combination, including Evelyn.

After opening the safe, she put the bag on a shelf and took out the ring once again. It was dark in the safe, so she stepped into the room and inspected the ring under the antique lighting. A brilliant oval rose cut ruby sparkled in the center. It had to be at least three carats with smaller diamonds encircling it and was set in a thick silver band. Evelyn had educated herself about antique jewelry when she and James had been looking for engagement rings. With their love of history, they had both wanted something old and unique. They had settled on a WWII-era ring, much like her mother's ring.

"Knock, knock," a woman's voice met Evelyn's ears a moment before Joy Atkins poked her head into the Vault. "I heard about the ring. Oh, is that it?"

Joy was the manager of the hospital gift shop. Since news traveled fast at Mercy, Evelyn wasn't surprised to see Joy—or Anne Mabry, another friend and volunteer extraordinaire at the hospital, who stepped into the room right behind Joy.

"I ran into Shirley when I was dropping off a bouquet of flowers to one of the nurses in the ER," Joy said, her blue eyes wide with interest. "She told me about the ring and said you were putting it into the safe. I thought I'd come and see it since my shift just ended."

"I have it here." Evelyn held up the heavy ring. The ruby caught the light and sparkled.

Joy and Anne came closer to look at it.

"Do you think it's real?" Joy's dark hair was worn in a short and simple bob, which she often tucked behind her ears. She smelled like the candles she sold in the gift shop, and she was wearing a pretty earrings and necklace set she more than likely purchased through the hospital gift shop

"It looks real to me," Anne said in a distracted tone as she looked closely at the ring. She wore her blond hair a little longer, close to her shoulders. Though she was always dressed well, it was her perpetual smile that made Anne stand out in a crowd. No matter where she went, or what task she was given, Anne was often smiling.

"My goodness," Joy said. "It's immense."

"And old." Evelyn turned the ring in her fingers. "Do you see the band? It's made of silver, which was popular during the 1700s. And the rounded shape, with the flat bottom, is called a rose cut ruby. It was common from the 1500s up to the 1800s."

"Does it have an inscription?" Anne asked.

Evelyn turned the ring over and rotated it in her fingers. "There is an inscription." She squinted and looked closer. "*LPOC*," she read.

"LPOC?" Joy frowned. "What does that stand for?"

"I don't know." Evelyn shrugged. "Maybe someone's initials?"

"It doesn't look as worn as you would expect for something so old." Anne reached out and lightly touched the ruby.

"I can't imagine it would be worn often," Joy mused, "especially in this day and age. Can you imagine how conspicuous you would feel walking around with this on your hand?"

"What about the woman who owns it?" Anne looked at Evelyn. "Do you know anything about her?"

Evelyn shook her head. "Just her name."

"I heard she is unconscious." Joy shook her head. "She had a serious head trauma from her accident. It could be days or weeks before she regains consciousness—if she ever does."

"Is she expected to live?" Anne asked.

"Shirley didn't tell me much." Joy lifted her shoulder. "But it doesn't sound good."

"We'll need to add her to our prayer list." Evelyn stepped into the safe and put the ring back into the bag.

"And we should add the man who caused the accident," Joy chimed in. "I heard he's pretty shaken up about the whole thing."

"Can you imagine the guilt?" Anne pressed her lips together. "Poor man. He must feel terrible about what happened."

The ladies were quiet for a moment, and then Evelyn stepped out of the safe and closed the door tight. "Did you know James purchased my engagement ring in an antique shop? Ever since then, old rings have intrigued me." She held up her left hand for them to see the WWII-era ring. "I like to think that the person who owned this before me had a long and happy marriage. Sometimes it's hard to learn the history behind jewelry, but when you do, it can be fascinating. I think I'll do a little research into the ring, just for fun. It's not every day we have something so beautiful come into Mercy."

"If you learn anything interesting," Joy said, "please let me know."

"And me," Anne added. "I'm sure there's a great story behind that piece of jewelry."

Evelyn followed the ladies out of the Vault and into the records department.

Joy glanced at the clock. It was past three, which was when she usually went home. "I'm off. I have a meeting this afternoon with my garden club. I'll see you two tomorrow."

Evelyn and Anne waved at Joy as she left.

"And what about you?" Anne asked Evelyn. "Anything fun planned for after work?"

"I don't know." Evelyn shrugged. "James mentioned to me this morning that he had a surprise project he was going to work on today and that I needed to clear my schedule for this evening."

Anne's eyebrows rose high. "That sounds exciting. What do you think he has in mind?"

"I have no idea." Evelyn lifted her hands. "I'm completely clueless."

"Did he mention anything over the last couple of weeks that might give you an idea?"

"Nothing I can think of. I've been racking my brain all day, and still nothing. But he seemed very excited, so I've been kind of excited all day too."

Anne smiled. "Now you've got me excited. I can't wait to hear about it."

"I'm sure I'll have lots to tell you in the morning." Evelyn's desk phone started to ring.

"I'll let you go. See you tomorrow."

"Bye." Evelyn waved at Anne and then took a seat at her desk.

She still had a couple of hours of work ahead of her, but the reminder of James's surprise had her wishing she could go home early. What in the world could he be up to?